"What happ

"I've arranged [armed] guards. You should be safe here, and the sooner you can retrieve your memories, the better."

The weight of his words, coupled with the fear that raced through her momentarily, left her speechless. Colette stared at the handsome man before her. Even though she had no specific memories of her time with the Swamp Soul Stealer, when she thought about it, fear tightened the back of her throat and made it difficult for her to draw a full breath.

Now Chief Savoie was asking her to retrieve those details to find the kidnapper who might be a killer as well.

As she gazed into Etienne's smoke gray eyes, she wanted to pull up those memories and hand them to him. But she couldn't. She simply didn't have them right now to give to him.

"I promise I'll give you all my memories as they come back to me," she replied fervently.

He reached out and took her hand in his. "Colette, we'll get through all this together."

HUNTED IN THE REEDS

CARLA CASSIDY

INTRIGUE

Harlequin®
INTRIGUE™

ISBN-13: 978-1-335-69007-4

Hunted in the Reeds

Copyright © 2025 by Carla Bracale

Recycling programs for this product may not exist in your area.

For questions and comments about the quality of this book, please contact us at CustomerService@Harlequin.com.

TM and ® are trademarks of Harlequin Enterprises ULC.

Harlequin Enterprises ULC
22 Adelaide St. West, 41st Floor
Toronto, Ontario M5H 4E3, Canada
www.Harlequin.com

Printed in Lithuania

MIX
Paper | Supporting responsible forestry
FSC® C021394

Carla Cassidy is an award-winning, *New York Times* bestselling author who has written over 170 books, including 150 for Harlequin. She has won the Centennial Award from Romance Writers of America. Most recently she won the 2019 Write Touch Readers' Award for her Harlequin Intrigue title *Desperate Strangers*. Carla believes the only thing better than curling up with a good book is sitting down at the computer with a good story to write.

Books by Carla Cassidy

Harlequin Intrigue and Harlequin Romantic Suspense

Marsh Mysteries

Stalked Through the Mist
Swamp Shadows
Hunted in the Reeds

The Scarecrow Murders

Killer in the Heartland
Guarding a Forbidden Love
The Cowboy Next Door
Stalker in the Storm

Cowboys of Holiday Ranch

Sheltered by the Cowboy
Guardian Cowboy
Cowboy Defender
Cowboy's Vow to Protect
The Cowboy's Targeted Bride
The Last Cowboy Standing

Visit the Author Profile page
at Harlequin.com for more titles.

CAST OF CHARACTERS

Colette Broussard—She's afraid of her repressed memories and yet needs to remember in order to bring a madman to justice.

Etienne Savoie—He needs Colette's memories to catch the Swamp Soul Stealer, a man who has terrorized the people in the swamp and who has three men and three women in his lair.

Adam Soreson—He was behind a recall effort against Etienne. Is it possible Etienne is getting too close to the kidnapper and so Adam wants the investigation stopped?

Brett Mayfield—The handyman has a reputation for bar fights. Is it possible he's doing the unthinkable in his spare time?

Jason Maynard—The computer repairman is extremely bright and known to be a loner—both characteristics Etienne believes fit the Swamp Soul Stealer.

Chapter One

"It's okay, Colette. You're safe here. Nobody is going to hurt you again. You can wake up now."

The deep, rich voice penetrated the darkness that surrounded her. Colette Broussard listened to the familiar voice that called to her. This wasn't the first time he'd spoken to her.

He would talk to her, and then there would be silence once again, and then he would come back to talk to her some more. "Colette, honey, I need you to wake up now. Climb out of the darkness and open your eyes."

She wanted to please the voice, but there was still a deep fear inside her. She wasn't sure exactly what she was afraid of, but there was safety in the darkness, and so she clung to it tightly.

Then he was gone again, and there was nothing but silence. The next time he came, once again he assured her that she was safe, that nothing was going to hurt her again, and she needed to wake up. And once again she found herself wanting to please this man who had talked to her so many times before…the person who had been an odd kind of comfort in the perpetual nighttime of her world.

This time, instead of wrapping the darkness around her, she slowly climbed toward the light and cracked open her eyes. She immediately winced against the illumination in the room.

Her senses all went wild... The scent of disinfectant and the sounds of beeping and buzzing from a variety of machines that surrounded the hospital bed she was in created a cacophony of stimulus that was immediately overwhelming.

Finally, there was a handsome man with dark, curly hair and gray eyes. Still, his features were fuzzy as her eyes tried to adjust to the light.

He grabbed her hand and smiled at her. "Good morning, Colette. It's so good to see you here with me. I'm just going to go get the doctor, okay?" He released her hand and walked out of the room.

She looked around frantically. What was she doing in the hospital? How had she gotten here, and what was wrong with her?

As she tried to remember why she was here, a headache bloomed across her forehead, and she just wanted to close her eyes and escape into the safety of the darkness once again.

However, before she could slip away, a man with gray hair and wearing a doctor's coat entered the room followed by several female nurses. "Hi, Colette," he said with a kind smile. "I'm Dr. Dwight Maison. We've been taking care of you while you've been asleep."

She frowned. "H-how long..." Her voice felt scratchy, and her mouth was exceedingly dry. One of the nurses got her a small cup of water from the sink in the room, and she drank it greedily, the cold liquid sliding down to soothe her dry throat.

She looked at the doctor once again. "How long have I been asleep?"

"We'll talk about all that after I check your vitals," he replied.

As he listened to her heart and the band around her arm pumped up to take her blood pressure, she wondered what had happened to the man with the voice. Who was he? And where had he gone? Had he only been a figment of her imagination?

"Now, how are you feeling?" Dr. Maison asked as he sat in the chair next to her bed.

"I have a bit of a headache, but other than that I'm feeling okay. I'm just not sure why I'm here. Was I in some sort of car accident?" she asked in confusion.

Dr. Maison looked at her in surprise. "Uh...what's the last thing you remember?"

She frowned thoughtfully. "I remember working late into the evening writing an article, and then I decided to make a quick run to the grocery store. I wanted to get some eggs for breakfast the next morning." Her frown deepened. "I remember leaving my shanty, and... I... uh... That's the last thing I remember. So how did I get here?"

"Colette, you were kidnapped and held by the Swamp Soul Stealer."

She stared at him. It was as if he had suddenly started speaking in a foreign language. "Kidnapped," she echoed faintly. "The Swamp Soul Stealer?"

"That's the name the newspapers have given him.

He's kidnapped five people besides you, and nobody knows if those other people are dead or alive. Somehow you must have managed to escape him, and you were found at the edge of the swamp. You'd been beaten and starved, and we immediately put you into a medically induced coma so you could heal."

A half-hysterical burst of laughter escaped her. It sounded so outrageous. "Why don't I remember any of that?"

"It's possible your mind is protecting you right now from those memories, and they'll eventually come back to you," the doctor explained.

"So how long had I been kidnapped?"

He hesitated a long moment. "Almost three months," he finally replied.

Once again, she stared at him, not knowing whether to scream or cry. Three months? How was that even possible? "And how long have I been here in the hospital?"

"You've been here with us for almost three months," he replied.

Six months? She'd lost six months of her life, and in that time, she'd been beaten and starved, escaped from some kidnapper and then been put to sleep? Oh, how she longed for the comfort of the darkness right now.

Dr. Maison placed a hand on hers. "I know this is a lot for you to take in, but, Colette, we've got you healthy again, and you have survived it all. You are a very strong and brave woman."

At the moment she didn't feel strong or brave. She was overwhelmed by everything he had told her. Her headache intensified as she struggled to understand it all.

"Was…was I raped?" she asked, almost afraid of the answer.

He smiled at her kindly. "We saw no signs of sexual assault when you were found."

Thank God, she thought in relief. It was crazy that she'd been beaten and starved, but being sexually assaulted would have upset her the most.

"When can I go home?" Surely, she would feel much better once she was back in her shanty and amid her familiar things.

"First thing in the morning, we'll remove your feeding tube and other things and then I'd like to keep you for another two days or so to make sure you can hold food down and your bodily functions return to normal." He stood. "And now, since it's the middle of the night, we'll just leave you to rest until morning. If you need anything at all, hit the button for a nurse and somebody will come in. It's wonderful to see you awake, Colette."

"Thank you, Dr. Maison," she replied even though she was disappointed that she'd have to stay here for another couple of days. What's another couple of days when she'd already lost six months of her life, she thought half hysterically.

Minutes later she was alone in the room and still grappling with everything she had just learned about herself. No matter how hard she tried to remember anything from the last six months, those memories remained elusive.

Maybe it was better if she never remembered the time she'd been held by a kidnapper.

She wished the man with the voice would come back

to assure her everything was going to be okay and that she was safe. Maybe he had been some sort of a guardian angel sent to help ease her from the darkness to the light.

As she closed her eyes, she imagined him talking to her now, soothing and comforting her through the darkness of her life.

CHIEF OF POLICE Etienne Savoie paced the small confines of the hospital waiting room. September's early-morning sunshine flooded through the nearby windows as he waited for Colette's release.

She'd been awake now for three days, but Etienne hadn't seen her since the night she'd first opened her eyes. The doctor had refused to allow her any visitors while she adjusted to being awake and all that came with it.

Dr. Maison had called Etienne earlier that morning to let him know that Colette was being released. He was hoping Etienne would take the woman home since she had no family to pick her up.

Etienne had been champing at the bit to talk to Colette. He was hoping she could tell him about the man who had kidnapped her. The Swamp Soul Stealer had managed to kidnap two women and four men without leaving any clues behind. Hopefully, Colette held all the answers as to the identity of the man.

Etienne had hoped that the other victims were all still alive since Colette had been found after three months of captivity. But she'd been barely clinging to life when she was found, and Etienne worried that a clock was ticking for all the missing.

He stopped his pacing as Dr. Maison came out to greet him.

"Chief," the doctor said with a nod of his head.

"How's our girl? Is she ready to get out of here?" Etienne asked.

"She's definitely ready to leave, but I need to talk to you about something important before you take her home."

"Something important?" Etienne looked at the older man curiously.

"She doesn't remember anything."

Etienne frowned. "What do you mean?"

"She has no memory of her captivity. The last thing she remembers is deciding to go to the grocery store and then waking up here, but she remembers absolutely nothing in between."

Etienne stared at the doctor in surprise and more than a little bit of dismay. "Is this...uh...amnesia normal in these kind of circumstances?"

"I've done some research into it, and yes, it can be quite normal."

"Is it permanent?" For the past three months, Etienne had hoped and prayed she would awaken and have enough information that he could make an arrest. The disappointment that swept through him now was all-consuming.

"Actually, it may not be permanent. I believe right now Colette's mind is protecting her from remembering all the trauma she went through. Once she feels safe and strong enough, it's very possible her memories will start to return."

Etienne felt a little better about the situation. His job would now be to make sure she felt safe and supported. He desperately needed her memories to do his job as chief of police and catch the man who was terrorizing the swamp.

"She should be ready for release any minute now. My nurses gathered up some clothes for her to wear home since she had nothing of her own. I'll just go get her for you." The doctor turned on his heels and disappeared through the double door marked DO NOT ENTER.

Etienne found himself ridiculously nervous to interact with the sleeping beauty he had sat next to and talked to night after night. Of course, she wouldn't know that. But during those nights, as crazy as it sounded, he had felt a strange connection with her.

The door reopened, and Colette walked out. She was clad in a pair of slightly baggy black sweatpants and a blue T-shirt. Her long dark hair was held at the nape of her neck with a large gold barrette. She was still too thin and looked incredibly fragile, but there was no question that she was a beautiful woman.

Dr. Maison walked by her side, and when they reached where Etienne stood, the doctor introduced her to the lawman. "Chief Savoie has offered to take you home and see that you get settled in okay."

Etienne had wondered about the color of her eyes. He hadn't noticed in that moment when she first opened them. They were a beautiful dark chocolate brown with thick long dark lashes.

She gazed at him tentatively. "Thank you, that's very kind of you."

He'd also wondered what her voice would sound like and was oddly pleased that it was low and melodious. "Are you ready to go?" he asked.

She looked up at the doctor and then gazed back at Etienne. "I guess I'm ready."

"You're going to be just fine, Colette," Dr. Maison said with a warm smile. "Remember what I told you. You are a very strong and brave woman."

"Thank you, Dr. Maison. Thank you for everything," she replied and then looked at Etienne expectantly.

"My car is parked right outside the front door," he said and gestured her toward the exit. Together, they walked down the long hallway and out the hospital doors.

He opened the passenger side of his car, and she slid into the seat. He hadn't driven his patrol car to pick her up but had driven his personal vehicle instead, a dark blue sedan. He also wasn't in uniform but wore a pair of jeans and a navy T-shirt. However, he did wear his shoulder holster and gun, something he always did when he was out and about.

Once she was inside the car, he hurried around to the driver side and got in. He shot her a quick smile as he started the car. "How does it feel to be awake and finally leaving the hospital?"

"To be honest, it's all a little bit overwhelming right now."

"I can certainly understand that," he replied.

"I still can't believe I've lost six months of my life."

"Hopefully it won't take you too long to adjust and go forward from here." He glanced over at her once again.

She stared out the front window, an anxious expression on her pretty features. As if feeling his gaze on her, she turned and looked at him. "Thank you, Chief Savoie, for taking me home. I really appreciate it."

"No problem. I'm assuming I need to go to the big entrance of the swamp."

"Yes, and from there I can walk in to my shanty." Her anxious expression intensified. "Hopefully, it's still standing, and no squatter has taken it over while I've been gone."

"I'll be walking in with you to make sure everything is okay there," he assured her.

"I'd like to tell you that isn't necessary, but I'd really appreciate having you with me."

"Colette, I intend to be with you as much as possible as you transition back into your life. There's nothing more I want to do than support you."

He sensed her gaze on him once again. "Why?" she asked.

"Why? Because I know you have no family to see you through all this. Also, as chief of police, I feel responsible for everything you've been through," he replied. And there was the small fact that he needed her memories, but he certainly didn't want to tell her that... at least not yet.

For the next few minutes, they rode in silence. As he went down Main Street, he couldn't help but feel a strong sense of pride.

Crystal Cove, Louisiana, was a small town with lots

of heart. The buildings downtown were painted pink, yellow and turquoise, giving the town a special visual charm. The people here were warm and friendly. They were, for the most part, hardworking individuals who were always willing to lend a hand to help a neighbor.

Etienne took his job as chief of police very seriously. The fact that there was a man moving with impunity through the swamp and kidnapping people was beyond upsetting. He was still reeling with the information that Colette had no memories right now of her kidnapping. All he could hope for was that given a little time and getting settled back in her own routine, those memories would begin to return.

They reached the parking area where people who lived in the swamp left their cars. He pulled up and parked and they both got out of the car.

The swamp entrance in this area was like a big gaping mouth leading into a dark and mysterious jungle of tangled greenery. Etienne had been in the swamp many times, especially since the kidnappings. He and his officers had searched and hunted the marshland for the monster preying on the people who lived here.

They took several steps forward on a narrow path, and she suddenly stopped. She drew several deep breaths and then visibly relaxed.

"This I remember," she said softly. "The smell of greenery and flowers and just a faint hint of decaying fish." She offered him a bright smile that unexpectedly warmed him. "It's the fragrance of home."

"Then it must feel good to be back here," he said as they continued walking.

"It feels very good." She led him up one trail and then onto a narrower one. As it began to disappear, the sun still fought to shine through the large leaves of the cypress and tupelo trees overhead. Spanish moss dripped from some of the trees, the lacy patterns glittering when the sun found them.

The sound of fish jumping and the splash of gator tails came from pools of water nearby, and small animals scurried to get out of their way as they continued walking.

They passed several other shanties. He had been to one of them not that long ago when somebody had tried to kill Angel Marchant.

Angel, a strong, beautiful woman who lived in the swamp, had met and fallen for Nathan Merrick. Nathan was a writer/photographer who was working on a book about the flora and fauna in the swamp. Angel had agreed to be his tour guide, and as the two of them worked together, they had fallen in love. However, that had stirred a jealous rage in one of her male friends who believed she belonged to him.

One night, Louis Mignot attacked Nathan, hitting him over the head and rendering him unconscious. Louis then confronted Angel in her shanty. His love for her had turned to a deadly rage, and he attacked her with the intention of killing her. In the end, Angel managed to stab Louis, ending his life.

Etienne had been there to investigate and clean up the crime scene and to assure Angel that she had done the right thing. Thankfully, she and Nathan were happy together and were now planning a wedding.

At least that case had a happy ending, he thought as they passed by Angel's shanty. Colette led him up another narrow path, and then after several more minutes of walking, a shanty came into view.

It was like most of the other ones in the area. Built of wood and on stilts over a large expanse of water, it had several windows and a wraparound porch. A wooden rocking chair sat on the porch by the front door, as if just waiting for her to come home and sit a spell.

"At least it's still standing," she said as they walked across the narrow bridge that led to the front door. Once she got there, she grabbed the doorknob and then turned and frowned at him in dismay. "It's locked, and I don't have the key."

"Is there a back door?" he asked.

She brightened. "Yes, and a lot of times I would forget about locking it."

"Then, let's go check it out." He led her around the porch and to the back door. The knob turned easily. He drew his gun and went in before her, just in case somebody had decided to move into the shanty while she was missing.

He took several steps inside and then stopped and listened. The house held the complete silence of vacancy. He turned back to her. "It's safe to come in," he said as he holstered his gun.

She followed him in, and they went through the small kitchen and on into the living room.

"Does everything look like it's supposed to?"

She looked around and slowly nodded. "Yes, it does."

"Why don't you sit tight here, and I'll just check out the rest of the place?" he said.

She nodded and sank down onto the dark brown sofa with its bright yellow throw pillows. There was an overall brightness to the living room with a matching brown chair and a small desk and accents of yellow all around. It was quite a warm and attractive space.

He stepped into the bedroom where a double bed was covered with a bedspread filled with sunflowers. A nightstand held a battery-operated lamp, and a dresser with a mirror was against one wall.

He checked the closet to make sure nobody was hiding there and then walked across the hall and checked out a small bathroom that only had a sink and a stool. He had learned that most of the shanties had outdoor showers that ran with rain and bottled water. Everything inside ran on complicated systems of water that he knew little about.

With the space entirely checked out, he went back into the living room and sat on the sofa next to her. "No human critters hiding anywhere," he said with a smile.

"Thanks, and looking around, I don't see anything that's missing. I guess I've been very lucky."

"You know what I think? I believe the people here in the swamp have great admiration for you as a survivor, and they're hoping you can help me catch this Swamp Soul Stealer."

"But I can't help you. I don't remember anything to help you," she said, her eyes appearing to darken.

"I'm hoping that will change in time," he replied.

At that moment, a knock sounded on her front door.

Etienne stood as Colette got up from the sofa and answered. It was Ella Gaines who worked at the café. Immediately, the two women hugged.

"Oh, Colette, it's so good to see you alive and well," Ella said as she released her hold on Colette. The two women sank down onto the sofa.

"How did you know I was home?" Colette asked.

"You know how the grapevine around here works. The minute you stepped into the swamp, people started talking," Ella replied.

"Well, I'm happy to see you," Colette said.

"You've gotten far too thin," Ella continued. "I'm going to have to fatten you up with some of my deluxe cornbread and big fried shrimp."

"That sounds good to me," Etienne quipped, making the two women laugh.

Ella sobered and grabbed Colette's hands. "Oh, I've missed my best friend."

"And I've missed you," Colette replied.

There was another knock on the door, and more people arrived to visit. There was Jaxon Patin, who was Colette's closest neighbor. Then there was Layla and Liam Guerin, Hudson Decuir and Levi Morel, all friends and neighbors of Colette.

They pulled in chairs from the kitchen, and Jaxon and Levi sat on the floor, while Etienne stood by the front door and just watched the interactions going on.

"Have you told Chief Savoie who the Swamp Soul Stealer is?" Levi asked. He was a big guy with broad shoulders and thick thighs. Etienne knew he was a gator hunter, as was Jaxon Patin.

"Unfortunately, right now I have no memory of my time in captivity," Colette replied.

"For real? You don't remember anything?" Levi asked.

"Nothing," she said.

"That doesn't matter, we're just happy you're back here safe and sound," Layla said with a reassuring smile.

"Seriously, you don't remember anything at all?" Levi pressed, his dark eyes gazing at Colette intently. "Not a single thing?"

"Levi, knock it off. She already answered you," Ella said with a glare at the man.

"I just wanted to be sure that she has amnesia," Levi replied. "I've never known anyone who had it before."

"Well, now you know somebody," Colette replied with a smile.

It was at that moment Etienne realized an important issue he hadn't considered before now. He'd initially believed that Colette would be able to give him enough information to make an immediate arrest in this case. The Swamp Soul Stealer would be caught and put into jail, and nobody would have to worry about him again.

Unfortunately, it hadn't happened that way. And now Colette would be in even bigger danger from the monster who had kidnapped her.

The Swamp Soul Stealer would eventually hear that they were waiting for her memories to come back to her. He would want to get rid of her before that happened. With this thought in mind, Etienne stepped outside and made a phone call to the station to make some arrangements, and then he returned to the living room.

As he watched her talk and laugh with her friends, he realized she was in imminent danger. He wanted her memories, but his real job now was keeping her alive so she had the time to retrieve them.

Chapter Two

It was late afternoon by the time all her friends left, and Colette was positively exhausted. Ella was the last to leave, and once she was gone, Colette turned and smiled at the handsome chief of police.

"Chief Savoie, thank you so much for all your time today," she said as she sat back down on the sofa.

"Please, make it Etienne," he said and sank down next to her. "You seem to have a nice group of supportive friends."

"They're all great. Most of them I've been friends with since we were young kids," she replied.

Etienne Savoie was a very handsome man with strong, bold features. His dark curly hair begged a woman's fingers to dance through it, and his dark gray eyes held streaks of silver like the wings on a blackbird. He reminded her of somebody, but she couldn't remember who.

He smelled as good as he looked. His cologne was spicy and rich and threatened to pull her in, but the last thing she needed right now was a crush on the chief of police. She had plenty in her own life to figure out without adding issues.

"We have a few more things to talk about before I leave," he said.

"And what's that?" she asked curiously. Right now, what she really wanted to do was get something to eat and then veg out on the sofa until bedtime. Her first foray back into real life had been positively exhausting.

He gazed at her soberly. "We both know that you have no memories right now to help me make an arrest in the Swamp Soul Stealer case. Eventually, this man is going to hear that we're waiting for your memory to return."

She frowned. "Okay… I'm not sure what you're saying."

He leaned toward her. "I'm saying that I believe you are now in danger from the Swamp Soul Stealer. He's going to want to stop you before you can give me any information that might lead to his arrest."

She stared at him as a new horror crept through her. Of course, he was right. She just hadn't had time to process everything yet. "So what happens now?"

"I've already arranged for armed guards to sit on your porch. You should be safe here, and if you need to go anywhere, call and let me know, and we'll see what we can do. Meanwhile, the sooner you can retrieve your memories, the better. You helping to identify this creep will get him under arrest, and then nobody will be in danger from him again."

The weight of his words, coupled with the fear that raced through her momentarily, left her speechless. She stared at the handsome man before her. Even though she had no specific memories of her time with the

Swamp Soul Stealer, when she thought about it, her general reaction was an abject fear that tightened the back of her throat and made it difficult for her to draw a full breath.

Now Chief Savoie was asking her to retrieve those details to find the kidnapper who might be a killer as well.

As she gazed into Etienne's smoke gray eyes, she wanted to pull up those memories and hand them to him. But she couldn't. She simply didn't have them right now to give to him.

"I promise I'll give you all my memories as they come back to me," she replied fervently.

He reached out and took her hand in his, his touch holding an odd familiarity and a wealth of comfort. "Colette, we'll get through all this together," he said reassuringly. He pulled his hand back and stood. "And now I'm sure you're exhausted. You've had a long first day, and I'm also sure you're more than ready to be alone and really get settled in here."

"I am tired," she admitted and rose to her feet as well. Her brain struggled to process everything she'd been told since opening her eyes three days before. There was no question that it all was overwhelming.

They walked to her front door, and Etienne opened it and gestured to a uniformed officer seated in the rocking chair. The officer smiled at her and waved.

"Colette, this is Officer Joel Smith. He'll be sitting on duty outside here for the night."

"Thank you," Colette said to the officer, once again overwhelmed by everything that was happening.

"And I'll check in with you sometime tomorrow," Etienne said. "Now get some rest and enjoy being home."

With that, he left, and she was finally alone in her shanty. She walked from room to room as her brain bubbled with one thought after another.

Apparently, she had been kidnapped and held by somebody for three months. She'd been found half-dead and then had been in a coma for the next three months. As if that wasn't enough, the man who kidnapped her could possibly still be a threat to her life. And the cherry on top of it all was the fact that she was suffering from amnesia. Could her life get more complicated?

Since it was getting dark, she went around the room and lit the battery-operated lamps she had. She was thankful they all still worked. She then collapsed onto the sofa and looked around.

This room had always been her sanctuary. It was both her workspace and her relaxing place. As she looked at the small desk against one wall, she thought about what she'd been doing months ago before she had been kidnapped and her life had been so disrupted.

She had been a fairly popular blogger and had also been writing and selling articles about swamp life to a couple of magazines. She could only assume after her six-month absence she'd lost those jobs and her blogging business as well.

In the next few days, she'd see if she could pick back up where she'd left off. She'd write a few articles and offer them to the magazines she'd sold to before.

She got up from the sofa and went into the kitchen

where she found a packet of tuna that hadn't expired and a box of crackers in her food cabinet. She sat at the kitchen table to eat them. She definitely needed to get some groceries. Everything in her cooler had gone bad. Thankfully there hadn't been a lot in there.

Once she was finished with the tuna and crackers, she quickly cleaned the cooler out. But that wasn't the only thing that had caught her attention as she'd walked through the shanty earlier. Every piece of furniture was covered with a fine layer of dust.

Tomorrow would be a cleaning day. Tonight she was just too tired to worry about any of it.

Even though it was relatively early, she decided to call it a night. She turned out all the lanterns and then went to her bedroom. The bed beckoned to her, and she quickly changed into a clean nightshirt from one of the dresser drawers and then fell into the soft mattress.

Almost immediately her brain filled with all the stress she had going on in her life. It was all so overwhelming, like a bad dream. Only she wouldn't easily awaken from it. It was definitely disconcerting to know there was an armed guard just outside her door. It was especially upsetting to know the guard was there because another man might try to kill her.

Still, it wasn't long before the sounds of frogs croaking and crickets chirping filled the night. Soft bird calls and the white noise of the swamp slowly relaxed her and lulled her to sleep.

SHE AWAKENED THE next morning, surprised that it was after nine. She dressed for the day and then went out to her back porch to start her generator. It had lain dormant for six months. She breathed a sigh of relief when it started right up.

She went back inside, made herself a quick breakfast and then moved to her little desk in the living room. She dusted everything off, turned on her laptop and began perusing files, trying to familiarize herself with what she might have been working on before her kidnapping.

Work was the best way she knew not to dwell on everything else in her life. She'd always been able to completely immerse herself in her writing, and today was no different.

She jerked to awareness as a knock fell on her door. Instantly, a knot of fear formed in the back of her throat. She suddenly remembered there was supposed to be an armed guard outside. She peered out the front window and saw Etienne with several bags in his hands.

A quick look at the clock as she hurried to the door let her know it was just after noon. She had definitely lost track of time while working.

He was clad in a pair of jeans and a light blue polo that displayed his broad shoulders and taut biceps. He looked incredibly handsome, and as she opened the door, his smile warmed her from head to toe.

"Afternoon, Colette," he greeted her.

She opened the door wider to invite him in. "Good afternoon."

"I took the liberty of picking up some things for you at the grocery store. I suspect your cupboards are probably pretty empty."

"They are," she admitted. "Please, bring them in."

She led him to the kitchen where he set the bags on the small wooden table.

"It's mostly just staples…bread, milk, eggs, with a few other items. I would prefer you not go to the grocery store right now, so I figured while I'm here you could make me a list and I can bring the things to you this evening. I'll be back here on guard duty. There's a block of ice in this bag. I knew your cooler would need that." He pulled out the ice and placed it in the back of the large cooler that served as her refrigerator.

She began to empty the other bags he'd brought with him. "I really appreciate all this. You need to tell me how much you spent so I can repay you." Thank goodness the jar of cash she kept had been right where it was supposed to be, hidden away in the bottom of her closet. At least she had money on hand to pay him.

"Don't worry about it," he replied easily.

She put a carton of eggs in her cooler and then turned back to face him. "Oh no, Chief Savoie, while I appreciate your kind offer, I pay my own way."

"Okay, but I told you to make it Etienne."

She grinned at him. "Okay, then I pay my own way, Etienne."

"That's better." He smiled at her once again. Oh, the man had a wonderful smile. It crinkled the corners of his amazing eyes and lit up all his features.

"So, how did it feel to sleep in your own bed last night after being gone from it for so long?"

"It felt wonderful. In fact, I slept later this morning than I ever remember doing before." She put the last of the grocery items away and then gestured for him to follow her back into the living room.

He sat on the sofa and she settled in a chair facing him. "How are you feeling this morning?" he asked.

She knew what he really wanted to know. "I'm sorry, but no memories have come to mind yet."

"I really was just asking about you, not your memories," he chided gently. "You look better rested today than you did when I left you last night."

"Getting some extra sleep definitely helped, and I've had a nice morning. I spent the morning writing, and it felt good to be back in the saddle, so to speak. Before all this happened, I wrote articles about swamp life, and I had a fairly successful blog."

"That's interesting," he said, his gray eyes curious. "Do you sell the articles you write?"

She laughed. "That's the general idea. I used to sell to several magazines, and I had a nice following. Of course, a six-month absence means I'll be starting all over again now."

"That's unfortunate, but hopefully it won't take you too long to get back to where you were."

"And hopefully it won't take me too much time to remember things that can help you in your pursuit of this soul stealer man."

His eyes narrowed slightly. "So far, the man has been like a damned ghost who leaves nothing behind. But now that you mention the whole memory thing, I've been thinking of ways we might possibly jog your memory."

The muscles in her stomach instantly tightened. "What have you come up with?"

He leaned forward. "We believe this man is holding his captives somewhere here in the swamp. My officers and I have searched, but we've been unsuccessful in finding the lair. I was thinking maybe you and I could take some walks through the swamp? Might jog something loose in your memories about the location."

The idea of walking in search of the place where a monster lived, a monster who had held her for three long months and had nearly killed her, caused a new fear to tighten up the back of her throat. "Wh-when would you want to start this?"

He gazed at her for several long moments, obviously hearing the abject dread in her tone. "We'll wait a couple of days until you feel a little stronger."

She felt as if he'd handed her a small reprieve, but more than ever she knew she needed her memories to return to her. The only problem was, she was almost as afraid of those memories as she was of the monster who was after her.

ETIENNE LEFT THE swamp with a grocery list in hand and thoughts of Colette weighing heavy in his mind. She'd looked so much better today. Far more relaxed and obviously comfortable in her own space. Clad in a pair of jeans that had hugged her slender legs and slim hips and a light pink T-shirt that clung to her breasts, she had stirred something unexpected…something raw and hot inside of him.

He needed to keep his relationship with her strictly

professional. However, those nights of sitting with her while she'd been in her strange slumber had somehow connected him to her in a nebulous way. He didn't understand it, but he felt it.

He headed straight to the police station, wanting to check in before he headed home for a few hours of sleep. He had guard duty tonight and needed to make sure he'd be alert through the entire night.

He parked in his space behind the police station and went in through the back door. The hallway was empty as he headed to his office. Once at his desk, he quickly checked his emails and notes to make sure nothing demanded his immediate attention.

He'd just finished up when a knock fell on his door. "Enter," he called.

Trey Norton came in. A tall, fit dark-haired man, he was Etienne's right-hand man.

"Hey, Chief," Trey greeted him and took the chair in front of Etienne's desk.

"What's up?" Etienne asked.

"Nothing much. What about with you and our sleeping beauty? Anything exciting and new on that front yet?"

"I wish. So far, she's remembered nothing. I'm going to give her a few days to relax and get comfortable. If nothing changes, I'm going to start trying to push her." He told Trey about his idea of taking Colette for walks in the swamp. "I'm also going to suggest she get some therapy with Dr. Amber Kingston. From what I've heard, she's a great therapist. Maybe she can help Colette retrieve some of her repressed memories."

"Sounds like a good plan to me. Hopefully it will work," Trey said. "I heard through the grapevine that you were taking the night duty at her place."

"Yeah, and I'm going to be depending on you to hold things down here during the days ahead. I'm planning on coming in for a couple hours each day, but I need to work in some downtime so I can be awake all night for guard duty."

"Got it," Trey replied. "You know you can depend on me."

Etienne grinned at his friend and coworker. "If I couldn't depend on you, then you wouldn't be my assistant chief. Instead, you'd be emptying all the trash cans and cleaning out the jail cell bathrooms."

"I'd much rather be your assistant chief," Trey said with his own grin. "Is there anything specific you need for me to do today?"

Etienne released a tired sigh. "Actually, there is something. I'd like Levi Morel's alibis checked for the nights of the disappearances. He seemed far too interested in what Colette remembered when he was visiting with her yesterday. He lives in the swamp, but I'm not sure where. If you talk to some of Colette's neighbors, I'm sure they can tell you where his shanty is located."

"Levi Morel... Got it. I'll get on it this afternoon," Trey replied.

"He's probably nothing more than an overly curious friend, but still, I'd like him checked out," Etienne said.

"I'll see what I can find out about him."

"Good. I'm going to head home now and get a couple hours of sleep."

"Etienne, I know how heavy these whole Swamp Soul Stealer crimes have weighed on you," Trey said. "We all hope Colette will remember some crucial clues that will get the man under arrest and the people he's kidnapped free."

"I just hope and pray those people are all still alive." Etienne released another deep sigh. "I have to consider the possibility that Colette might never remember anything that will help us."

"All we can do at this point is hope this guy makes a mistake and leaves us some clues to follow," Trey replied.

"Yeah, well, so far that hasn't happened." Etienne raked a hand through his hair in frustration. "Have you heard anything more on the recall effort?" A small knot tightened in his belly.

For the past couple of weeks there had been some rumblings around town about a recall for his position. Some people had become unhappy that this crime hadn't already been solved. They had become disillusioned with Etienne and believed somebody else could handle the job better.

"Etienne, that recall isn't going to go anywhere," Trey replied. "It's just a handful of loudmouths leading the charge. Most of the people here still strongly support you."

"We'll see," Etienne said and stood. "I think I'll go ahead and head home now."

Trey got up from his chair and walked to the office door with Etienne. "Then I guess I'll see you sometime tomorrow."

"Yeah, I should be in around 8:30 a.m. I've got J.T. coming on guard duty at the shanty at eight in the morning."

Together, the two men left the office and went in opposite directions.

Trey was a high school buddy, and Etienne had been pleased when he'd joined the police department six years before. At that time, Etienne had been twenty-seven years old and had just become the chief of police in the small town.

In the past seven years, Etienne had devoted himself to the job. He'd rarely dated, but lately he did find himself a little lonely. However, it was something he didn't dwell on. Besides, he'd been too busy trying to solve the Swamp Soul Stealer case to focus on much of anything else.

His house was about fifteen minutes from the police station in a nice neighborhood. It was a modest three-bedroom ranch that he'd bought two years ago. An added benefit was that it was only a block away from where his aging parents lived.

As he pulled into the garage, a weighty exhaustion rode on his shoulders. For months, he'd found sleep nearly impossible. The Swamp Soul Stealer case had tormented him, haunting his sleep with nightmares and the cries of victims.

Once Colette had been found, his sleepless nights had been spent with her. He'd watched her cuts and bruises slowly heal and her body put on much-needed weight. Through her transformation, he'd talked to her as he sat with her night after night.

During those times, he spoke to her about anything and nothing. He recounted his days for her and told her his dreams to eventually have a wife and fill his home with the sound of little feet and laughter. He'd also told her that he hadn't found that special someone yet and wasn't sure he ever would. In truth, he'd decided that he was a man destined to live alone with his work as his wife and family.

Once Colette had been pulled out of her medically induced coma, he'd spent each night trying to get her to wake up. He doubted that she'd been aware of him, but the moment she opened her eyes, he'd been filled with a tremendous joy. It came from more than the answers he needed from her to solve a crime. It was the sheer joy that a woman so broken had successfully survived her ordeals.

The minute Etienne was inside his house, he dropped his wallet, keys and utility belt on the end table next to his black recliner. Lately, he spent as much time sleeping in this chair as he did his bed. It often felt like far too much trouble to get into bed with the lack of sleep he got.

And, if he was perfectly honest with himself, he'd admit that it was that edge of loneliness he felt that kept him from the big bed that begged for two bodies.

Even though he knew it probably wasn't necessary, he set an alarm on his watch to wake him for his night duty. It was going to be a long night. He planned on being at Colette's place at seven and would remain there until eight the next morning.

He had taken the long hours of the night shift mostly

due to a lack of manpower and the fact that he believed if the man came after her, it would be during the darkness of night. And he wanted to be the one to get the bastard. He wanted that so badly.

He must have fallen asleep for he awakened at five, feeling refreshed and ready for the night to come. He took a quick shower and then dressed in a clean uniform. Strapping on his utility belt and gun, he then grabbed the grocery list Colette had given him earlier in the day and left his house.

His first stop was at Big D's Burgers, a drive-through where he ordered a cheeseburger and quickly ate it in his car. Then he was off to the grocery store.

Maynard's Grocery was located in the middle of Main Street. It did a brisk business as it was the only grocery store in town, and today was no different. The parking lot was nearly full as Etienne pulled in.

Colette's list was fairly short…some meat and fresh vegetables. He was greeted pleasantly by the other shoppers and in no time at all, he was headed for the swamp.

It was 6:45 p.m. when he parked at the swamp's entrance. He grabbed the bags of groceries and strode into the marshland.

He hoped the kidnapper made a move on Colette tonight. Etienne's blood heated at the very thought. He'd told his officers to keep quiet about the guards at her house. Hopefully, the Swamp Soul Stealer would believe Colette was alone and vulnerable in her shanty.

Thankfully, he remembered the way to her place.

When he arrived, Joel, who had been on duty during the day, stood from the rocking chair.

"Evening, Chief," Joel greeted him.

"Evening, Joel. Everything quiet?"

"Has been all day," the officer replied. "She did have one visitor. Layla Guerin stopped by and brought Colette some fresh fish and a couple of potatoes. I stopped her at the door and brought the items in to Colette and that was the only person who's been here."

"Thanks, Joel. Now, go on, get out of here and get yourself some dinner," Etienne said.

"Linda will have a nice meal waiting for me," Joel replied. Joel had been dating Linda Michaels for the past year, and two months ago she had moved in with him.

"Well, enjoy it," Etienne said.

"Have a good night, Chief," Joel said. He crossed the bridge and disappeared into the encroaching twilight shadows and the tangled greenery.

Etienne knocked on Colette's door, surprised as a small edge of excitement shot through him. He told himself it was just because he was hoping she had remembered something since he'd last seen her, but the truth of the matter was he looked forward to seeing her again.

Strictly professional, he reminded himself. No matter that she stirred him in a physical way that no other woman had before, he had to keep their relationship professional.

At that moment she opened the door. "Etienne, come in," she said with a smile that instantly warmed him.

"I brought you the groceries you ordered," he said

as he followed her into the kitchen. The air smelled of freshly fried fish.

"Great, let me just get them put away." She took the bags from him and set them on the table.

"How was your afternoon?" he asked as she began putting the meat into the cooler. The fresh vegetables and fruit she pushed to one side of the small counter.

"It was pretty quiet. I spent most of the time doing a little housecleaning. Everything was so dusty, and I was just glad to get rid of all of it."

She offered him another one of her lovely smiles. "I'm just getting ready to sit down and eat a little dinner. It isn't anything fancy, just some fried fish and potatoes, but I'd love it if you'd join me."

He shouldn't sit at her table and enjoy a meal with her. It would blur the lines between them. However, he wanted her to be completely comfortable with him. He needed to support her through this journey to regain her memories.

In this particular case, he realized, he had to blur the lines. He needed to get as close as possible to her as a friend and yet ignore the fact that he was incredibly physically drawn to her.

"I'd love to have some dinner with you," he finally replied.

Her responding smile lit him up inside and made him realize just how difficult a task he'd set for himself.

Chapter Three

Colette was ridiculously pleased that he'd agreed to eat with her. He looked incredibly handsome in his official blue uniform, and she couldn't help the way her heart warmed in his presence. "Please sit," she said, gesturing him toward the small table. "It's ready right now."

"It certainly smells good," he replied as he sat.

She set silverware on the table and then set two plates next to the skillet so she could fill them. Thankfully, the fish Layla had brought her that afternoon was a good size. There were several big pieces.

She placed one of the bigger ones on a plate for Etienne and added a bunch of diced browned potatoes. She brought it and a plate for herself to the table.

Even though the fish smelled good, Etienne smelled much better. His attractive, slightly spicy cologne mingled with the faint scent of shaving cream and a fresh-scented soap.

"Can I get you something to drink? I have water, or I could make a pot of coffee," she offered.

"No, I'm good," he said with a smile. "Sit down and relax. I'm ready to dig into this."

She sat in the chair opposite him. "Then let's."

"This is absolutely delicious," he said after taking his first bite.

"Thank you." Her cheeks warmed at his compliment. "The breading on the fish is my mother's recipe."

"Do you enjoy cooking?" he asked.

"I do, although I usually don't go to too much trouble when it's just me. What about you? Do you cook or do you have somebody at home who cooks for you?" It was hopefully a subtle way for her to learn if he had a significant other in his life or not.

"The only person who occasionally cooks for me is my mother. I've got no wife and no girlfriend, but sometimes my mom will take pity on me and bring me some of her home cooking," he replied.

"Oh, that's nice." What was really nice was the fact that he was single. "So you're close to your parents?"

"Very close. I'm their only kid, so it's always been just the three of us. In fact, I now live just a block away from them, and we often visit with each other." He frowned. "At least we did before this whole Swamp Soul Stealer case came along. For the last few months, I haven't had much spare time to visit with anyone."

"I could help with that if I could just remember anything," she said in frustration.

He reached out and lightly stroked the back of her hand. The simple touch sparked something exhilarating and breathless inside her. It only lasted a moment as he pulled his hand back from hers. "Colette, I know you're doing the best that you can," he said.

"To be honest, I'm a little bit afraid of my memories," she confessed.

"Afraid? Why?" He looked at her curiously.

"Because I know they are filled with horrors. Dr. Maison told me about the condition I was found in. So I'm a bit afraid to revisit them."

"Those horrors can't hurt you anymore. You survived everything that happened to you, and that part of your life is now over. It can't hurt you anymore. None of your memories can harm you."

She stared at him for several long moments, slowly digesting his words. Of course, he was right. Whatever horrors lived in her brain couldn't hurt her. She had survived whatever she had been through with the monster who had held her.

"Thank you. You've just made me feel a lot better," she said.

He grinned at her. "Good."

His smiles should be illegal. It was ridiculous the way they made her feel. Unfortunately, his smile quickly fell away. "I'm sorry you don't have your parents with you, especially now while you're going through all of this. I'm sure it would help you if they were here."

A familiar grief stabbed through her even though it had been three years since she'd lost them. "I had a bad feeling the morning they left here to drive to New Orleans for their anniversary," she said. "They had so many fun plans for that weekend. So excited to get away." A touch of anger rose up inside her. "All drunk drivers should be arrested and put into jail for the rest of their lives."

"What happened to the man who hit your parents' car?"

"He was charged with two counts of manslaughter and received a sentence of three years. In the next couple months, he'll be back out on the streets living his best life, but my parents are gone forever."

"He got a ridiculously light sentence," Etienne said.

"His parents are wealthy, and he had a good defense team. But enough about that," she insisted. "We'd better finish eating while it's all still warm."

"I can tell you right now that I definitely intend to clean my plate," he replied.

For a few minutes, they ate in a comfortable silence. She had to remind herself that he was only here because he was on guard duty.

Despite her attraction to him, she'd do well to remember he wasn't here because he was attracted to her or because he was eager to spend time with her on a personal level. He was doing his job and just happened to accept her invitation to a meal.

"I'm curious, would you be interested in getting some therapy?" he asked once they had finished eating.

"I could probably use some, and I'm certainly not averse to the idea."

"We have a good therapist right here in town. Her name is Dr. Amber Kingston, and she does FaceTime appointments."

"I would definitely be interested in that. Tomorrow I'll look her up and see what we can arrange," she replied. After a six-month absence from her life and with a case of amnesia, it certainly wouldn't hurt to get some therapy.

"I was also wondering how good your memory is for the time before you were kidnapped," he replied.

"I think I remember everything up until I decided to make a late evening run for groceries," she replied. "I wanted to get eggs for breakfast the next morning. Instead, I got kidnapped."

"Okay, enough about your memories," he said and stood. "Now tell me how I can help with the dinner cleanup."

"That's easy. You can't help," she said firmly as she got up from the table.

"Well, thank you for the meal," he said. "It was definitely the highlight of my day."

"And thank you for the company. It was the highlight of mine," she replied. They walked together to her front door.

He stopped at the door and turned to look at her. His smoke gray eyes held a wealth of sympathy. "I imagine it's going to be a bit lonely for you since we aren't letting anyone come in or you out until we get this guy behind bars. At least you had one opportunity to visit with your friends when you came home from the hospital before we changed the rules."

"It will be a bit lonely, but I'll survive," she replied. Her work as a writer forced her to be alone a lot of the time, but there was no question that before all this happened, she'd been a social person. Rarely did a day go by that somebody didn't stop in to visit or she went out with her girlfriends.

"As long as you understand that I'm doing all this to keep you safe," he said.

She smiled. "Trust me, I understand."

"On that note, I'll get out of here and let you enjoy the rest of your evening. Thank you again for the unexpected and wonderful meal."

"I'm just glad you enjoyed it," she replied. And then he was gone, swallowed up by the darkness of the night as he left the shanty.

She locked the door behind him and went back into the kitchen to clean up. As she worked, her thoughts were filled with the man who had just gone outside.

It was surprising that he didn't have a wife or a significant other. With his dark, slightly curly hair and his beautiful gray eyes and bold chiseled features, she couldn't imagine a single woman in town who wouldn't want to claim him as her own.

She certainly didn't know him well at all, but there was no question she was physically drawn to him. A single touch from him had ignited a surprising flicker inside her. When he gazed at her, she wanted to fall into the warm gray depths of his eyes. She couldn't remember ever having such a visceral reaction to a man before.

Even though she didn't know much about him, she felt a strange comfort when he was around. It was more than just the fact he was a law officer in charge of her safety, but she couldn't explain it.

But no matter how attracted she was to him, she was just a job to him. She had to remember he wanted nothing more from her than her memories, and she was going to do her very best to give him what he wanted as soon as possible.

Hopefully, the therapy would help her retrieve her lost memories and the bad guy would end up in jail. The only downside was that would be the end of her time with the handsome lawman.

ETIENNE SAT IN the darkness, listening to the sounds of the swamp all around him. Frogs croaked their deep-throated songs, and small nocturnal animals rustled through the brush. He was hoping for a much bigger animal to show up.

There was no question in his mind the Swamp Soul Stealer would come after Colette. Ettienne knew it was just a matter of when.

Everyone in town now knew that Colette didn't have her memories...yet. That information had flown around like wildfire as everyone wanted the monster caught. Even though the crimes had taken place in the swamp and only affected the people who lived there, everyone in Crystal Cove wanted these crimes solved and the perpetrator arrested.

Etienne frowned and touched the butt of his gun as he thought about the man he sought. Four men and three women had been plucked from their lives and apparently taken someplace to be starved and abused. Why? He couldn't even begin to guess at the motivation for such a crime.

It was obvious from the condition that Colette had been found in that the victims were being treated horribly. Again, why? Etienne and his team had checked the backgrounds of all the victims to see if they intersected in any way by somehow angering or having issues with a specific person. There was nothing there, nothing obvious to tie the victims together.

So who was this monster and what was his end goal? Why was he kidnapping these people? Where in the swamp was he hiding these four men and now just two women? Was it somebody who lived in the swamp or somebody who lived in town?

There were certainly far more questions about these crimes than there were answers. He still hoped many of the answers resided in Colette's brain and she'd be able to access them soon, but only time would tell.

Meanwhile, he and his men would continue to investigate anything that came up in an effort to find the Swamp Soul Stealer and his victims. Etienne prayed that all the victims were still alive.

He didn't have to worry about falling asleep. Even if he wasn't on guard duty, it would have just been another sleepless night in his recliner.

As the night deepened, the shanty emitted a soft glow, letting him know Colette had turned on her lanterns in the living room. About an hour after that, all the lights went out, and he knew she'd gone to bed.

Colette. He was shocked by his intense physical attraction to her. Never before had a woman affected him on such a primal level. Was it all mixed up because of her importance to his case? He didn't know. What he did know was it was something that wouldn't and couldn't be explored. He had to do everything in his power to tamp down his desire whenever he was around her. She had enough to deal with in her life.

A deep guilt swept through him as he thought of her

and her memories. He was asking her to recall what he knew would be horrible things. Right now, there was a soft innocence about her, but once she pulled back the veil and remembered her time in captivity, she would probably lose that softness.

He'd lied to her when he told her that her memories couldn't hurt her. He knew they could... They would deeply hurt her. While she had survived her time with a monster, remembering everything that had been done to her by him might break her forever.

He was a lawman who needed her memories to catch the monster, but he was also a man who didn't want her to have to suffer. It was definitely a challenging situation.

The night deepened, and the swamp darkened. From his vantage point, a small break in the trees overhead allowed him to see a slice of the sky. Stars winked their brilliance in the otherwise dark canvas of the night.

It was hard to believe that in all this primal beauty, a monster stalked in the night. Hopefully most of the swamp people now knew the dangers of going out of their homes after dark. What surprised and perplexed him was that it was not just vulnerable women who had been taken, but also strong young men. As crimes went, this one was confusing.

The night slowly passed, and dawn began to paint the area with a golden glow. It was just after 6:30 a.m. when the sound of Colette's generator thrummed in the air, letting him know she was awake.

At a few minutes before seven, her door opened, and she stood just inside the doorway. He stood from the rocking chair and greeted her. She was clad in a long, coral-colored robe and held a cup of coffee out to him. The color of the robe was amazing against her dark beauty.

"Good morning," she said. "I thought you might be ready for coffee. I don't know how you like it, so right now it's just black."

"Just black is exactly the way I like it," he replied, touched by her thoughtfulness. He took the cup from her and couldn't help but notice her scent. She smelled like a fresh exotic flower. It was a fragrance he found very appealing. "Thank you. It's very kind of you."

"It's the least I can do for a man who spent his night outside in a rocking chair guarding me," she replied. "Do you want to come in to drink it?"

"No, thanks, I'll just drink it out here. It won't be long, and I'll be off duty. But thanks again."

She nodded, offered him a smile and then closed the door. Etienne returned to his seat in the rocking chair. The strong dark brew was welcome, and as he sipped it, he watched the dawn finish its brilliant dance across the sky.

He drank all of the coffee and knocked on her door to return the cup. By that time, J.T. Caldwell appeared to take over watch duty.

J.T. was young with a baby face that emphasized his youth. The other officers teased him about being the baby on the squad, but he was a damn good officer who loved what he did.

Etienne greeted him with a smile. "You ready for this? It's going to be a long day."

J.T. held up a canvas bag. "I have a couple of peanut butter and jelly sandwiches, a thermos of hot coffee and a soda in here. I'm ready to take on the day," he replied with a boyish grin.

"Then I'm going to leave you in charge here, and I'll see you this evening," Etienne replied.

"See you then," J.T. replied cheerfully.

Minutes later Etienne was in his car and headed to the police department. He was eager to see if Trey had managed to connect with Levi the day before.

Levi was a big man, accustomed to wrestling with gators. He would have the strength needed to take down a victim and then carry them off to wherever his den was located. Still, the only thing that had raised Etienne's suspicions about the man was the way he questioned Colette about her memories when all the friends had been together at her house.

He was one of few men who had raised any suspicions at all since the beginning of the kidnappings. Etienne knew it wasn't much to go on, but right now he would leave no stone unturned in the hunt for the Swamp Soul Stealer and his victims.

As usual when he entered the police station through the back door, the hallway to his office was empty. Most of the officers on duty would be out on the streets. There was always an officer at the front desk, and Trey should be there as the top officer when Etienne was away.

As he sat at his desk, thoughts of the victims played in his mind. Luka Lurance was a good-looking young man. He was lean and fit and had been one of the first people to just vanish into thin air.

Then there had been Colette, Haley Chenevert and Sophia Fabre, all taken in fairly quick succession. Haley was the youngest of the three at twenty years old, and Colette had been the oldest at twenty-eight.

Finally, there was Willie Trahan, Clayton Beauregard and Jacques Augustin. At first it had been believed that Willie got his nose in some moonshine and stumbled off somewhere in the swamp to sleep it off. He'd been known to do that on occasion. But when he hadn't returned to his shanty two days later, the worst was believed.

Clayton Beauregard had left his young wife and newborn son to make a quick run to the store for formula. When he didn't immediately return, his wife called Etienne. He and a couple of his men had gone to Clayton and Lillie's place and discovered grocery bags not far from their shanty but no sign of Clayton. It was heartbreaking how close Clayton had been to the safety of his home when he was taken.

Jacques Augustin had disappeared in the last two weeks. He was a slender man with a pleasant personality who fished for a living.

Mothers, fathers, wives and friends had all cried on Etienne's shoulders, terrified and grief-stricken by the disappearance of their loved ones. Their tears and fear filled Etienne's heart with a heaviness he thought might never go away.

Dammit, he didn't care about the recall effort that might oust him from his job. If the people of Crystal

Cove had lost their confidence in him, then he needed to go for the good of the town he loved.

But not quite yet. This was a job he had to finish. He wanted to be the lawman to catch the man who had terrorized the people of Crystal Cove and haunted his sleep for the past five months or so.

Somewhere along the line, this had become personal to him. Now, more than anything, he wanted to catch the man who had tortured Colette so badly. He desperately wanted to capture the man who had nearly killed her and put the dark shadows into the depths of her beautiful eyes.

These thoughts snapped away as Trey appeared in his office door. "Just the man I was going to go find," Etienne said and gestured Trey into the chair in front of his desk.

"Long night?" Trey asked.

"Yeah, but I managed. Tell me what's new here," Etienne said.

"Joel and I caught up with Levi Morel late yesterday afternoon," Trey said.

Etienne leaned forward, any tiredness from the long hours of the night before momentarily gone. "And?"

"And he was definitely not happy to talk to us. He said he was deeply offended that we would even think he had anything to do with the kidnappings."

"That doesn't surprise me," Etienne replied. "Of course that's what he would say."

"He had damn little in the way of alibis for the nights of the kidnappings. He couldn't remember what he was doing and assumed he was out in the swamp hunting gators all alone. Or he was in his shanty alone."

"So no real alibis," Etienne said thoughtfully.

"Do you really think he's a viable suspect?"

Etienne thought about the big man who had pressed Colette so hard about her memory on her first day home. "He's certainly big and strong enough to carry bodies around."

"And as a gator hunter, he would know places in the swamp that we wouldn't," Trey added.

"I think he's a potential suspect," Etienne replied. "Why don't you see if we can get Judge Cooke to give us a search warrant for his shanty? Even though we don't have any real evidence against Levi, hopefully the judge will see things our way and grant the warrant."

"I'll get to work on it right away," Trey said.

"Call me when you hear something," Etienne said, his weariness back to weigh heavily on his shoulders. "This might all be a crapshoot, but it's one I want to follow up on. Maybe we'll find something in his shanty that incriminates him."

"It would definitely be good to have an end to this case," Trey said.

"It would be better than good," Etienne replied.

What would be really great was if they could solve these crimes without Colette having to revisit the horror of her memories.

Chapter Four

Colette turned the two pork chops browning in her pan. She'd already made skillet cornbread and had a bowl of coleslaw in the cooler.

It was just before seven...about when Etienne would come on duty to guard her. She was wearing a pair of jeans and a pink sleeveless blouse she knew looked good on her. Her long thick hair was pulled back at the nape of her neck with a pink tie.

She hoped the handsome lawman would come in to eat with her again tonight, but she really had no idea if he would or not. If he didn't, she would just have leftovers tomorrow night.

She told herself she would welcome anyone coming into the shanty for a visit. Really, she just wanted Etienne to come in because she was a bit lonely. Besides, he wasn't coming to her shanty for a friendly visit. He was coming here because he was on guard duty, keeping her safe from a man who wanted to kill her.

But that didn't explain the little dance of pleasure inside her heart as she thought about spending more time with him. There was no question that she was intensely drawn to him, and it had nothing to do with the fact that right now he was her only connection to the outside world and he was protecting her from some unknown monster in the swamp.

She turned down the heat of the electric stovetop beneath the skillet. Then she made sure the table was clean and ready for company.

At a couple minutes before seven, a wave of nervous energy swept through her as she walked to her front door. She unlocked and then opened it.

He sat in the rocker, a handsome blue knight keeping her safe from all harm as the sun was setting. He smiled at her and a wave of warmth filled her chest. "Evening, Colette," he said.

"Good evening, Etienne. I have some dinner ready in here if you'd like to join me."

"I'd love to join you," he said without hesitation. He rose from the rocking chair, and she opened the door wider to allow him in. As he walked past her, she once again smelled his scent. It was one of clean male and spicy cologne.

"Come on in and have a seat. I've got it ready to serve," she said.

He sat at the table, and she felt his gaze on her as she filled their plates with the pork chops, coleslaw, mashed potatoes and the golden-brown cornbread.

"You know you don't have to cook for me every evening," he said as she placed the plate before him. "Although this all looks and smells delicious."

"I really don't mind making a little extra each evening," she said and sat opposite him with her own plate. "Besides, I enjoy your company."

"And I enjoy yours," he replied with the smile that always warmed her in a way she couldn't explain.

"Well, let's eat while it's hot," she suggested. He'd said he enjoyed her company, but was it simply because he needed something from her? Was he just being kind to her because he needed her memories? Or did he truly enjoy her company?

She decided at that moment she wasn't going to overthink things with him. She enjoyed his company and intended to continue to do so until her memories returned or the Swamp Soul Stealer was caught and placed behind bars.

"This is all really good," he said after taking several bites.

"Thanks. My father always liked pork chops, although fried fish was his very favorite," she replied.

"Was he a fisherman?"

"He was." She smiled at thoughts of her dad. "He was a quiet man who loved fishing, my mother and me. He sold his fish to the people in the swamp who couldn't, for whatever reason or another, fish for themselves. There were many in the swamp who depended on my dad for their dinner each night."

"They must miss him then," Etienne replied.

She nodded. "I'm sure they do. So, how was your day?" she asked, wanting to change the topic and not dwell on the heartache that came from the loss of her parents. If she thought about it for too long, she could still cry over the loss of them.

He took a bite of the mashed potatoes and then washed it down with the bottle of water she'd set on the table. "Interesting," he finally answered, his gray eyes thoughtful.

"Interesting how?" she asked curiously.

"I think we finally have a new suspect in the Swamp Soul Stealer case."

She stared at him, her heart jumping with excitement. Was it possible he'd found the perpetrator without having her memories? That would be beyond amazing. "Oh, that's wonderful. Who is it?" she asked eagerly.

"I'm sorry, but right now we're keeping the information close to our chests," he replied and then frowned. "I probably shouldn't have even brought it up."

"But maybe if you told me who it is, it would jog something loose in my head," she said, still excited about the prospect of a new suspect.

He shook his head. "If I did that, then a defense attorney would have a field day and could argue I put things into your head. I'm sorry, Colette. Like I said, I probably shouldn't have said anything about it."

"I understand," she replied, although she was a bit disappointed that he wouldn't tell her the suspect's name. "Still, it's exciting that you have a new suspect. Maybe you can catch the man without me."

"I won't lie, Colette. It would be much easier to make a case if we had your memories to help us," he replied, his eyes the soft gray of a late twilight sky.

"I know… I'm really trying," she replied fervently. "I've been thinking about it almost all the time." It was true. In the quiet hours of the day, she'd tried over and over again to bring forth the memories that were trapped inside her mind.

"Maybe you shouldn't try so hard," he suggested. "Maybe you just need to relax about it, and then something will come to you when you least expect it."

"That's what Dr. Kingston told me today. I called her this morning, and we had a nice talk. We set up a Face-Time every other day for the next two weeks."

"That's great. So you connected with her," he replied.

"Definitely. I felt an instant connection with her, and I think we're going to work together just fine. Now, let's talk about something else."

He offered her one of his beautiful smiles. "How was the rest of your day?"

Once again, a sweet heat swirled through her. "It was pretty good. I got some more writing done, and I was happy with what I wrote. That always makes it a good day."

"Tell me more about this series you wrote about swamp life."

She laughed. "Oh, surely you don't want me to bore you with all that."

"I wouldn't find it boring at all," he replied. "I'm interested in it."

She was vaguely surprised and pleased that, though they had finished eating, he seemed to be in no hurry to leave the shanty and go outside. Rather he was lingering for more conversation with her.

"I started writing the articles to educate others about the people who live in the swamps. The general consensus has always been that the swamps are filled with drunks and lowlifes and criminals. I wanted to shine a light on the hardworking and good people who live here."

For the next fifteen minutes or so, she talked about the articles she had done in the past. She had written about everything from the people to the lifestyles and the beauty of swamp life. She had also detailed the dangers of living in a place where all kinds of wild animals existed.

"I'm so sorry," she finally said with an embarrassed laugh. "I've been rambling on and on."

"Please don't apologize. I enjoy listening and learning more about you and what you find important," he replied. "It's obvious you're passionate about what you do, and it's also obvious you love it here."

"I do love it here, but keep in mind I don't know anything else," she replied.

"Would you ever consider living in town?" he asked.

She frowned thoughtfully. "I don't know. I've never really thought about it before. I guess it would depend on a lot of things."

"I was just curious if it would be difficult for people who live here to transition from swamp life to town life," he replied.

"Lots of people have successfully made the transition," she said. "You're a town guy through and through, aren't you?"

"I am, but I have to be because of my job, although I might not have that for too much longer." His eyes darkened and a frown deepened the lines across his forehead.

"Why?" she asked in surprise.

"I've heard that there's a recall petition making the rounds."

"A recall? But, why?"

"I guess there are some people who aren't very happy with the way I've been conducting the investigation into the Swamp Soul Stealer," he replied. "They think this should have been solved a long time ago."

"But you can only do what you can do. When I was in the hospital, I heard that this man was like a ghost, stealing people without leaving any clues behind. How can anyone expect you to solve a case without any leads or clues?"

"I've done everything I can so far to catch this perp," he replied, his eyes appearing to grow darker.

"I'm sure you have," she replied, indignant on his behalf. "Let the person who started the recall petition solve the crimes. Let's see how far they get catching the monster."

He grinned at her. "I must say, I appreciate your support."

"Well, you definitely have it," she said fervently. "I was a victim of this monster. Of all the people who should be upset about the investigation, it should be me. But for years I heard what a good lawman you are, and I know you've been working hard on this case."

"Thank you, Colette. It's easy to forget that for most of my years as chief of police, people were happy with me and my team and the work we did to keep the peace in Crystal Cove."

"Etienne, you can't let this case define you." She reached out her hand and grasped his, wanting him to feel supported. His fingers curled around hers as if seeking her touch.

"I know," he replied. He squeezed her hand and then pulled away to rake the hand through his black, curly hair with a deep sigh. "I appreciate the meal and the pep talk," he said.

"A pep talk will be available anytime you need one, Etienne. There will also be a meal ready for you every single night for as long as you're on duty here," she replied.

"You know that isn't necessary," he said as he rose from the chair.

"I know, but I do enjoy your company, and I will enjoy cooking for us." She also got up from the table. "So it's settled. Every night dinner is on me."

"That's really nice of you, Colette."

"It's the least I can do for the man who is sitting at my front door through the hours of the night," she replied.

Together, they walked to the front door and just like the night before she was sorry to see him leave to sit in a chair in the dark. She was sure they were long hours for him, and she knew the only reason he was doing it was to protect her.

"Then I guess I'll see you tomorrow evening," he said when he reached the door.

"Etienne, I just want to tell you how much I appreciate what you're doing for me," she said as she placed a hand on his forearm.

He took a step toward her, and for a long moment they stood intimately close to each other. The air suddenly snapped with an electricity that also sparked inside her.

His dark gaze appeared to focus on her lips, and she leaned toward him. Her heart suddenly beat a quickened rhythm. Was he going to kiss her? Oh, it surprised her how much she wanted him to.

"It's my pleasure," he replied and jerked back from her.

She dropped her hand from his arm.

"Good night, Colette."

"'Night Etienne. I'll see you tomorrow." She closed and locked the door behind him. Leaning against the door, she relived the moment that had just happened between them.

She could have sworn she'd seen an impending kiss in his eyes. For a split second, it had shone bright and hot in those gray depths. And it had shocked her how much she wanted him to kiss her.

She shoved away from the door to start clearing the kitchen.

She hated the fact that Etienne seemed to be entertaining doubts about himself when it came to his job. She'd told him the truth when she said that before her ordeal, she had heard nothing but good things about the man who kept the law in Crystal Cove.

In all the years he'd held his job, she'd never had any interaction with him and hadn't even seen him except at a distance. Still, when he arrived at the hospital to take her home, there'd been an odd familiarity about him…as if they'd known each other for a long time.

Maybe her whole ordeal had made her more than a little crazy.

Even though she knew she was in danger, she felt no fear. With an officer guarding her through the day and Etienne on duty through the nights, she felt completely safe and protected.

Now, if she could just get her memories back, she'd be able to give them to Etienne so he could solve the crime. Knowing how he was feeling about himself made her want to retrieve them even more, though she was sure that would mean her time with him would end.

HE WATCHED CHIEF of Police Etienne Savoie go into the shanty, and his stomach twisted and churned tight with rage. He crouched low in the thick brush as he stared at the shanty where she was right now.

He'd thought the bitch was on death's doorstep when he took her back into the swamp to bury her. He hadn't intended to kill her, but he guessed he'd gone too far with her and she'd been too weak to survive. He was certain death was about to claim her, and he'd figured the best place to dispose of a body was deep in the swamp.

That night he had placed her on the ground next to him and began to dig a shallow hole to put her body in. All of a sudden, she sprang to her feet and took off running. It was so unexpected it took him a couple seconds to respond.

He'd chased after her, but the night and the swamp were so dark, he quickly lost track of her. He'd hoped she would collapse and die someplace in the tangled vines and thick brush. He was positively shocked when she was found the next morning.

He'd been scared as hell that she would be able to identify him. Thank God she'd been in such bad shape she was immediately placed in a medically induced coma. He prayed over and over again that she would never come out of it, that she would die in the hospital before ever awakening.

Then when she did, he learned she had amnesia. She couldn't remember him or what he had done to her. The amnesia was the only thing that was saving him...so far.

But she was still a danger to him. If her memories returned, she'd probably be able to identify him as the man who held her captive for three months, the man who had beaten and starved her.

There was no question about it, he had to kill her soon. She had to die before she started to regain any of her memories. It was obvious the cops knew she was in danger, as there was an officer outside of her door 24/7. But that wasn't going to stop him.

Somehow he'd figure out a way to get to her, and sooner rather than later.

"We got our search warrant for Morel's shanty," Trey said in greeting the next morning. "It just came in a few minutes ago from Judge Cooke."

Any tiredness from the night duty sloughed off Etienne's shoulders as a new adrenaline punched through him. "I'm surprised he bit since we had no real evidence to tie Morel to the kidnappings."

"I think the judge is as eager as we are to find the guilty party," Trey replied.

"Then let's get some men together and head out," Etienne said.

In the end it was Etienne, Trey, Joel Smith and Thomas Grier who loaded up in two cars and headed to the swamp to conduct a search of Levi Morel's shanty.

"It would be great if this pans out, and we find something from the victims inside Levi's place," Etienne said as he turned onto the street that would take them to the swamp's entrance.

"It would be better than great," Trey agreed.

"But it's possible this is just a wild-goose chase. It's also possible since he has the people in his control, he's not a souvenir taker." Etienne tightened his hands on the steering wheel.

"Still, it's something we need to check out. You told me that Levi really pressed Colette about her memory. Why would he care about it that much?"

"He definitely seemed to," Etienne replied. He looked in his rearview mirror where the other patrol car followed closely behind his. The four of them should easily be able to execute the search warrant.

As he drove, he couldn't help but think of the night before and his time with Colette. He'd enjoyed the meal and their conversation, but what surprised him was the fact that he'd nearly kissed her. He had wanted to take her lush lips with his and taste the fire he saw burning in her eyes. Thank God he had stopped himself before a kiss happened. He had a feeling if he started kissing Colette, he'd never want to stop.

He shoved thoughts of that moment away as he pulled into the parking area right before the swamp's entrance. Joel pulled his patrol car next to his, and together the four of them got out of the cars.

Adrenaline rushed through Etienne, quickening his heartbeat and flooding through his veins. Was it possible that this could be it? Could Levi be the one he sought? "We'll let Trey lead us in since he knows where Levi's shanty is located."

Trey nodded.

Etienne continued, "Be ready for anything. If this is our man, then he could be dangerous. Remember we need him alive to lead us to his captives. Besides, he might not be our man. Now, let's go."

Trey headed into the junglelike growth with the others following close behind him. Their path took them past Colette's shanty. Etienne saw Officer Michael Tempe seated in the rocking chair outside of her door, looking alert. He raised a hand and waved at them as they passed by.

The air was rich with the scents of greenery, mysterious florals and the ever-present underlying faint smell of decay. Little animals scurried from the trails in an effort to escape the human presence invading their space.

Not far from Colette's, they took a narrower path, and after a short walk, a small shanty appeared. Trey stopped walking and turned to the others. "That's Levi's place," he said quietly.

It was 9:30 a.m. Hopefully the gator hunter was home after his hunt or whatever it was he did during the night. Etienne moved in front of Trey and approached the front door. "Levi Morel," he called out as he knocked on the door.

They waited several moments for a response, and then Etienne knocked again, this time harder and louder. "Levi, it's the police. Open your door."

There was the sound of rustling inside, and the door flew open. It was obvious the big man had been in bed. His shaggy black hair was mussed, and he was wearing a pair of loose blue shorts and a stained gray T-shirt.

"What the hell is going on here?" he asked, his dark eyes blazing with irritation. "What the hell do you all want?"

"We're here to conduct a search of the premises," Etienne replied. He pulled the search warrant out of his pocket and handed it to the man.

Levi tossed it aside with a snort. "What gives you the right to come into my shanty and search?" He held the door tightly closed behind him with his big hand.

"That piece of paper you just threw aside gives us the right," Etienne replied. "Look, Levi, we don't want any trouble here. Just let us come in and do our job."

"So what are you looking for? Some kind of evidence that I'm the Swamp Soul Stealer?" Levi snorted again. "You all are crazy if you think I'm the one kidnapping people and holding them somewhere."

"Then let us come in to conduct our search," Etienne replied evenly. Interesting that the man had jumped to the conclusion that they were here about the kidnappings. "It won't take us long, and then we'll be gone and you can go about the rest of your day."

It was obvious Levi didn't want them inside his private domain. But no matter how much the man stalled and protested, Etienne was more determined than ever to get this done.

"Come on, Levi. I'd like to do this the easy way, but if you insist, we can do it the hard way. One way or another, it's getting done," Etienne said firmly.

Levi hesitated another long moment and then flung his door wide open and stepped outside. "Knock yourselves out. You stupid fools are completely wasting your time here."

Etienne motioned for Thomas to remain outside with Levi, and then he, Trey and Joel went inside. The first thing that struck Etienne was the smell. It was a combination of dirty laundry, gator and moonshine.

It was a small one-room shanty with a cot covered in ratty blankets pushed against one wall, a chest of drawers against another and the usual potbellied stove in a corner. There was also a three-shelf bookcase holding an overflowing variety of items. Dirty clothes formed a large pile at the foot of the bed. It was obvious Levi wasn't much into cleanliness.

"Trey, you check around the bed and go through the dirty clothes. Joel, look in and around the stove and then check out the drawers. I'm going to tackle this bookcase. Look for hidden compartments in the wood. Keep in mind if this is our guy, hopefully he's kept some souvenirs from the victims here. That's what we're looking for."

With that, the men all got to work. Etienne began to check the items on the bookcase. The top shelf held an open brown bottle. One sniff let him know that it was moonshine probably made by Jackson Renee Dupree, an old man who had a still somewhere in the swamp.

For the most part, the shelves held a lot of fishing items. Big hooks and spinners, broken reels and jars of stink bait filled up the space. What wasn't there was anything to tie Levi to the kidnappings.

"Nothing here," Joel said.

"Same here," Trey added in obvious frustration. "I went through the clothes one piece at a time, and it's obvious they all belong to Levi."

"Let's all look around the room and check the wood-work and the floor for any hidden compartments, then we'll go back outside and search the area around the shanty." Etienne released a deep sigh. The adrenaline that had initially pumped through him slowly began to depart.

Forty-five minutes later, they were finished with the search.

"I told you there was nothing here, because I'm not the man you're searching for," Levi said with obvious irritation. "You really got a problem with the case if you think I'm a good suspect. Now, get off my property and leave me alone." He returned to the shanty and slammed the front door shut.

Etienne and his men quietly made their way back to their vehicles. Exhaustion from his night duty and the disappointment from an unsuccessful search sat heavily on his shoulders.

"We knew it was a long shot," Trey said once they were in the car and headed back to the station.

"Yeah, I'd just hoped for a different outcome," Etienne said. "It's very possible our perp hasn't kept any souvenirs."

"That's absolutely possible. As long as he has the victims, he doesn't need the souvenirs. Unless another suspect pops up, I guess it's all up to Colette now."

Etienne frowned. He'd really hoped to do this without her. He'd hoped she would never have to remember her time in captivity when she'd been starved and beaten by some monster.

But now, it was more important than ever that she remember. What he feared was that in remembering, she'd be so traumatized she would never be the same again.

Chapter Five

For the past three nights, Etienne had shared dinner with Colette. The time with her had deepened their friendship and had also increased his physical draw to her.

She had told him over dinner that she'd had another session with Dr. Kingston, but no memories had returned to her yet.

He now sat in the rocking chair on the porch as the moon climbed higher in the sky. Insects buzzed and clicked, and frogs croaked their nightly songs.

There had been no breaks in the Swamp Soul Stealer case, but the dinners with Colette had definitely been enjoyable. They'd shared stories about their childhoods and had laughed together. He'd shared some incidents about various arrests he'd made, although he hadn't told her any names. She, in turn, had told him about funny times among the people in the swamp.

He found her not only beautiful and bright but also witty with a great sense of humor. His physical attraction to her was a constant battle he had with himself. He was desperate to maintain a close friendship with her but knew to explore a physical relationship with her was just plain wrong.

He didn't know how long he'd been sitting there with thoughts of Colette when he heard it…a slight rustling that came from the brush at the foot and to the right of Colette's short bridge. He grabbed the butt of his gun as a burst of adrenaline rushed through him.

The rustling got louder. Something…or somebody was definitely in the brush. He slowly rose to his feet, his heart beating a wild rhythm.

Would the Swamp Soul Stealer make so much noise? Did he want some kind of a showdown? If that was the case, then Etienne was ready for it. Dammit, he wanted this all over and done. He wanted Colette to be safe again and going about her life without the fear of some monster being after her. He also wanted the entire town of Crystal Cove to breathe a sigh of relief knowing the bad guy was behind bars and his victims had been saved.

He crept across the bridge, guided only by the faint moonlight overhead. He pulled his gun and held it steady in his hand as he moved closer to the rustling noise.

He kept his gaze divided between the moving brush and Colette's front door. It was only as he drew closer to the thick overgrowth that he heard a different sound. It was a series of snorts and grunts that immediately made him relax.

Beyond the brush was a small clearing, and in the clearing was a sounder of wild boar. The five big hogs rooted in the ground with their long snouts, overturning the soil and destroying the ground.

These wild beasts were a scourge in the swamp and

could be quite dangerous when confronted. With his gun still in hand, he broke through the brush and began to shoo them away. They squealed and snorted and thankfully didn't approach him, but ran off into the darkness.

Disappointed that it hadn't been an animal in the form of a man, he holstered his gun and walked back across the bridge to the rocking chair. As he eased back down, he thought of that moment when his attention had been divided between the moving brush and the porch.

He'd been lucky that it had been a bunch of wild boar and not somebody providing a distraction so another person could get through the front door and inside the shanty.

Was it possible the Swamp Soul Stealer was really two men working together? There had been no evidence pointing to that, but then again there had simply been no evidence at all.

In his heart of hearts, Etienne didn't believe it was two men working together. He and all his men believed these kidnappings were the work of one sick man. He could only hope that at some point the man would make a mistake and Etienne would be able to arrest him.

The rest of the night passed uneventfully, with thoughts of the monster in the swamp and Colette to keep him company. Early dawn was just streaking across the sky when the thrum of Colette's generator filled the air.

Twenty minutes later, the front door opened, and she stood there with a cup of coffee in her hand. Once again, she had on the coral-colored robe that looked so beautiful with her skin tone, black hair and brown eyes. "Good morning," she said and held out the cup to him.

He took it from her and grinned. "You're spoiling me, Colette."

She laughed, the sound musical and pleasant. "I enjoy spoiling you. Besides it's just a cup of coffee."

"Still, it is much appreciated," he replied and then sobered. "Colette, I'd like for us to take a walk through the swamp this afternoon. Would you be up for it?"

Any mirth that had been on her lovely features fell away. Her eyes appeared to darken, and her lower lip trembled slightly.

"Colette, I promise you'll be safe with me," he said softly in an effort to cut through the fear that radiated from her.

She slowly nodded. "Okay, I'm up for it. What time do you want to do this?"

"I was thinking maybe right after noon. That will give me a chance to check in at the office, and then I'll come back out here." He hated like hell to do this to her, but he was hoping a walk in the swamp might cause something to jog loose in that beautiful head of hers.

"Okay, then I'll be ready," she replied. "I'll just see you then." She stepped back inside and closed the door behind her.

He frowned and took a sip of the hot brew. He hated that he'd upset her. But something had to be done to try to retrieve her memories. He now believed it was the only way to catch the man he sought. Unfortunately, he had to sacrifice the one for the many.

Once his relief came, he left the swamp and headed into the office. For the next hour, he read over arrest reports for the last week, needing to keep up with what else was happening in his town.

A young man had been arrested for shoplifting at the convenience store. Five speeding tickets had been handed out, and Brett Mayfield had been taken into jail after another bar brawl at the Voodoo Lounge.

It wasn't the first time the big handyman had been arrested after a bar fight. Whenever Brett got drunk, he became belligerent and picked fights with other drunk people. Even when sober, Brett was a big mouth with a temper. Etienne had heard through the grapevine that Brett and a couple of his friends were behind the recall effort against him.

Once he'd read the arrest reports, he spent the rest of his time going over and over the notes from the investigation into the Swamp Soul Stealer. Somehow, someway, he kept believing they were missing something.

Finally, it was time for him to return to Colette's place. Despite his exhaustion, an edge of excitement lit up inside him.

Would this work? Was it possible just walking around the swamp would make her remember things… things that would identify the monster? He hoped this succeeded even though he dreaded her having to suffer any pain from the memories that might return to her.

If there was any other way to get an arrest, he would have done it. But the truth of the matter was that right now Colette was his last hope. The kidnapper could strike again at any time, and another person would just disappear from the swamp. Etienne wanted to get the man behind bars before that happened again.

He also knew as long as the Swamp Soul Stealer was out there, Colette was in danger. Etienne was vaguely surprised the man hadn't made a move on Colette yet.

He parked before the swamp entrance and went in. It didn't take him long to reach her place where Michael Tempe was once again on duty.

The officer sat up straighter in the rocking chair as Etienne approached him. "Hey, Chief," he said in surprise. "I didn't expect to see you at this time of the day."

"I'm here to take Colette for a walk. Even though she'll be gone from the shanty for a little while, I want you to sit tight here."

"Of course," Michael replied. "Unless you tell me otherwise, I'm on duty until you relieve me this evening."

"Good man," Etienne replied and then knocked on Colette's door. The door opened, and as usual, she looked beautiful. Her jeans fit her slender legs, and the red blouse she wore emphasized her light olive complexion and the rich chocolate of her long-lashed eyes. Her hair was a waterfall of rich darkness that fell down her back.

A wave of intense desire punched him in the gut as she offered him a tentative smile. "I'm ready," she said with a slight lift of her chin.

"Then let's take a little walk together," he replied.

She stepped out of the shanty, and he followed her down the bridge. When she reached the bottom, she paused and turned to him. "Which way are we going?"

"Why don't we start with what you remember from the night you decided to run to the grocery store for eggs?" he replied.

"From here, I walked toward the entrance of the swamp to get to my car," she said. Her features were tense with obvious stress.

He hated to see her this way. She had told him in one of their dinner conversations that her neighbors had not only taken care of her shanty while she'd been gone, but they'd also taken care of her car by starting it up every day so the battery wouldn't go dead.

"Then let's walk that way," he suggested.

She nodded, and together they began to walk slowly along the paths she'd taken the night she was kidnapped.

He watched her carefully. If he saw any indication that this was too much for her, then he would call the whole thing off. He also kept a close eye on their surroundings, wanting to make certain she was safe and there was nobody around to pose a danger to her.

It was a beautiful day. Bright sunshine broke through the trees and sparkled on the lacy Spanish moss they passed. Birds called from the tops of the trees, and it was hard to believe there was any evil here.

They hadn't gone too far when she suddenly stopped and slapped at the back of her neck. "It was here... I—I never heard him coming. Something stabbed into the back of my neck, and...and I went down. I... I can't talk... Can't scream. And then everything went black." She stared at him with wide eyes. "I remember, Etienne. I remember that moment when he drugged me."

He reached out and grabbed her hands. They trembled in his. "Who is it, Colette? Did you see his face?" he asked urgently.

She hesitated a moment and then slowly shook her head. "No… I'm sorry. I don't think I saw him then. He came from behind me, and I fell unconscious before I got a chance to see him."

"Still, this is good, Colette. You just gave me valuable information." They had suspected the victims were drugged, but it had just been a supposition up until now. Apparently, whatever drug he used was very fast-acting. This explained how he had claimed his victims.

"Maybe I'll remember more if we keep walking," she said, her eyes shining brightly with her success.

The desire to kiss her suddenly shot through him with a fierce intensity. He wanted to take her in his arms and press her body tight against his as he took her mouth with all the fire that was inside him.

Instead, he squeezed her hands and then released them. "Shall we walk some more?"

"Absolutely," she replied. She smiled, her eyes still glistening beautifully. "That was fairly easy."

"Yes, but we both know some of your memories aren't going to be so easy to retrieve," he reminded her. The memory she had just gotten had been fairly benign, but he knew how difficult and painful others would be for her.

Her smile slowly faded. "I know, but right now I'm feeling particularly strong and ready to remember."

He hoped so. He hoped this was just the beginning, and a rush of memories would return to her. And he wanted to be right next to her, supporting her as she delved into the horrid memories of her time in captivity.

COLETTE STOOD IN front of her two-burner stovetop and added a can of jarred Italian sauce to the browned hamburger in her skillet. In another pot, she had spaghetti noodles boiling.

As she cooked, she fought off a wave of discouragement. She had walked through the swamp with Etienne for about an hour and a half, but no more memories had returned to her.

Oh, she'd wanted to remember...for him...for Etienne. She'd wanted to gift him with the information that would put the kidnapper behind bars and free the other victims. She'd wanted to gift him in order to see his beautiful gray eyes light up and a smile of success curve his lips.

More than that, she wanted him to take her into his arms. She wanted his strong arms to surround her and his mouth to take hers in a kiss that dizzied her senses. The more time she spent with him, the more her desire for him grew.

As they walked through the swamp, he had been particularly attentive to her, asking her often if she was okay and obviously gauging her emotional health. She knew if she had shown too much stress, he would have immediately called the whole thing off and taken her back to her shanty.

There were times when she thought she saw desire in the depths of his eyes, but did he desire Colette the woman or Colette the person who had the potential to solve his case and save him from a recall? At this point she didn't know the answer.

With a deep sigh, she drained the spaghetti noodles and added it to the meat mixture. It was almost seven, and she was expecting Etienne to come in and eat with her as usual. Besides the spaghetti, she'd made skillet-browned garlic bread and intended to serve corn as well.

She was beginning to feel like a captive in her own home. The days were long without any social interaction at all. Was it any wonder she looked forward to these dinners with Etienne? It was the only conversation she had each day.

She didn't even have a phone to talk on. She had no idea where her purse had gone to when she'd been kidnapped. She had no driver's license and no identification. She hadn't had time to replace any of it before she went into protective custody.

At precisely seven, she went to the front door and opened it. As always, Etienne sat in the rocking chair, and he rose at her appearance.

"Good evening, Colette," he said with the smile that always lit her up inside.

"Evening, Etienne. Come on in, dinner is ready."

"Sounds good." He swept past her and she relocked her door, then followed him into the kitchen. He sat in his usual place at the table, and she began filling their plates.

"How was the rest of your day?" he asked.

"Quiet. What about yours? Did you get some sleep?"

"Yeah, I slept. This all looks good," he said as she placed his plate in front of him.

"It's nothing special," she replied, sitting across from him with her plate. "In fact, I need to give you another grocery list, and I need another block of ice for the cooler."

"You can give me a list tonight, and I'll bring the supplies tomorrow. Will that work?"

"Yes, that will work." She released a sigh.

He gazed at her for a long moment. "That was a very deep sigh. Are you upset about something?"

"No...not upset exactly." She picked up her fork, then set it back down. "I'm just starting to feel a bit like a prisoner here. While I love having you to talk to and eat with, I'm missing some social interaction during the long days. I'm really missing seeing something other than the four walls of my shanty."

He took a bite of the spaghetti, his gaze lingering on her. He swallowed and wiped his mouth with the paper towel she'd provided as a napkin. "Maybe tomorrow we can have lunch at the café and then go to the grocery store," he said.

"Really? Do you think it would be safe?" Her heart lifted at the thought of getting out of the shanty for an afternoon.

He frowned, obviously considering it. "I really can't imagine this guy would make a move on you out in public, so I think we can do this safely."

"Oh, I'd love to get out of these four walls for just a little bit of time," she admitted.

"Then we'll plan on lunch and the grocery store," he replied.

She gave him a huge smile. "Thank you, Etienne,

and I promise after tomorrow I'll go back to being a happy captive in this shanty."

He returned her smile. "I want you to be happy no matter where you are."

"For the most part I am happy," she said. Although she'd be much happier if Etienne would take her in his arms and hold her. She would be much happier if the lawman would take her lips with his and kiss her until she forgot everything that was going on in her life. The only time that happened was when she was writing, but she couldn't work all the time.

"When I'm working in here, it's easy to forget that somebody is after me and an armed guard sits on my porch day and night," she said, voicing her thoughts aloud. "To be honest, I'm surprised the Swamp Soul Stealer hasn't made a move to get to me yet."

"I'm a little surprised by that too. Still, we can't let our guard down," he said soberly. "I still believe you're at great risk from this man. You and I both know he'll be afraid of your memories and will want to silence you before they can return."

She released another deep sigh. "I know, but now let's talk about more pleasant things."

"Okay," he readily agreed. "So what's your favorite thing to order at the café?"

For the next hour as they ate, their conversation remained light and easy. They talked about the food at the café and then chatted about some of the stores in town.

When he talked about Crystal Cove, there was a real love of community that shone from his eyes and made him more handsome than ever. It was evident that he loved this little town. It would be a real sin if he was recalled and lost his job.

Once they finished eating, they lingered at the table, talking and laughing as they spoke about some of the more colorful boutiques in town.

"Have you been into Spiritual Haven?" she asked.

"Yeah, I went in to check it out when it first opened," he replied. "A bunch of nonsense if you ask me."

She laughed. "So you don't think crystals, herbs and astrology can change your life?"

"I don't, but apparently there are some people here in town who do. I've heard the store is fairly successful. What about you? Do you believe in crystal magic?"

"Not really," she replied. "But some of the crystals are quite pretty."

"Then there's the Voodoo Queens shop, have you been in it?" he asked.

She grinned. "I have. That store stands for much of what I try to dispel about people who live in the swamps. Spells and voodoo dolls aren't who we are, yet I've heard she sells a lot of her dolls." She released a small burst of laughter. "Heck, for all I know somebody has a voodoo doll out there with my name on it."

"I don't believe that," he scoffed and leaned back in the chair. "Tell me about the romances you've had in your life. Have you ever been in love?"

She blinked at the sudden change in topic. "When I was twenty-two, I dated a man who lives here in the swamp. We were together for about six months. I liked him and enjoyed spending time with him, but the relationship never really developed into anything deeper like real love. He was my only serious relationship, so the short answer is no, I've never been in love before," she replied. "What about you?"

"Kind of the same with me. When I was much younger, I dated a woman for about three months. Everybody said how perfect we were for each other, and I enjoyed her company. One day I realized I did love her, but I wasn't in love with her. I knew then that she wasn't the right one for me and that I was wasting her time, and so I broke up with her."

"How did she take it?" Colette asked curiously.

"Surprisingly well. In fact, within a month she was engaged to another man." He released a dry laugh. "I had assumed she'd cry into her pillow over me for at least a month, but I think she was almost as relieved as I was when I broke it off with her. What about your guy? How did he take it when you broke up with him?"

"He took it okay. Thankfully we managed to remain good friends," she replied.

"That's nice." He scooted back from the table, obviously ready to head to his post outside.

"I think that's the way it should always be," she said. "When two people part ways, there should be no reason for any acrimony between them."

"It would be nice if it always worked out that way," he agreed. "As usual, thanks for dinner," he added as the two of them got up from the table and then walked toward the front door.

"It's always the highlight of my day," she replied. As she walked closely next to him, his cologne seemed to wrap around her. The talk about romance once again stirred up her crazy desire for Etienne.

He paused at the door and turned back to face her as a fire danced in the very depths of his silver-gray eyes. She knew that fire... It heated the very center of her being.

For a moment, they were frozen in place, their gazes locked together, his body heat wafting toward her.

She leaned forward, mere inches from him. "Kiss me, Etienne." The words left her lips on a whisper of desire...of want.

His eyes flared even hotter, and he pulled her into his arms. His mouth captured hers in a kiss that immediately dizzied her senses as she wrapped her arms around his neck.

He pulled her closer, deepening the kiss. Their tongues swirled together in a heated dance, and she was lost in all things Etienne.

His body was so strong, so solid against her own, and she moved her hands across his broad back. She'd thought about being held in his arms for so long, and it was every bit as wonderful as she imagined.

He finally broke the kiss and stepped back from her. His eyes simmered with a wealth of emotions she couldn't even begin to discern. "I'm sorry, Colette. That should have never happened." His voice was deeper than usual.

"Why not? I wanted you to kiss me, Etienne," she replied softly. "In fact, I've been wanting it for some time now."

He frowned. "Well, it was a mistake, and it just isn't

a good idea. Trust me, it won't happen again. Now, I'll pick you up around eleven thirty for lunch tomorrow. I'll just say good night." He turned and went out the door.

She closed it behind him and walked back into the kitchen. Her lips were still warm with the imprint of his, and her heart still beat an uneven rhythm of desire.

It wasn't a mistake. The kiss had been inevitable. There was no question there had been a haze of sexual tension that swirled around the two of them since the moment he had brought her home from the hospital. It was a sexual tension that had grown bigger and hotter every day they spent together.

He'd said it was a mistake, but she'd tasted the desire in his kiss.

One thing was for certain, she was definitely falling for Etienne. Now not only did she have to worry about a monster trying to kill her...she also had to worry about getting her heart broken by the very man who was supposed to protect her.

Chapter Six

At 11:30 a.m. the next day, Etienne approached Colette's shanty. He'd had all night to think of the kiss he'd shared with her, and he still couldn't get it out of his head.

Her lips had been so soft and so inviting, and as her body had pressed against his, he'd become almost fully aroused. That had snapped him to his senses, and he'd ended the kiss.

She was a potential witness in a crime, a woman whose life was in his hands. She was vulnerable right now, and the last thing he wanted to do was take advantage of the situation or of her.

Still, even this morning as he thought about the brief but very hot kiss, he couldn't help wanting to repeat it. She was definitely a sweet temptation, but it was important that he be stronger than his desire for her.

His thoughts had also been filled with their outing today. He'd worked it from all angles, and he believed he could take her out and keep her safe. Surely the perp wouldn't be stupid enough to try to get to her in public where there would be witnesses everywhere. While taking her out of the shanty wasn't something he wanted to do every day, he'd give her today. He'd loved seeing her eyes light up with excitement at the possibility of the outing. He'd loved seeing her so happy.

As her shanty came into view, he couldn't help the small edge of anticipation that sliced through him. There was no question that he enjoyed spending time with her. He looked forward to the dinners they shared each evening.

Hopefully this outing would go off without a hitch. He understood her cabin fever, and he believed going to the café and the grocery store would be safe. As long as they were out in public, it should be okay.

He headed across the bridge and grinned at Thomas Grier, who sat on duty. "Hey, Thomas, I'm taking our girl out for a little while. Why don't you knock off here, go get some lunch and come back in about two hours?"

Thomas stood and stretched. "Sounds good to me. I'll see you in a little while."

Etienne watched as the man went down the bridge and disappeared into the green thicket. Etienne turned and knocked on the door.

She answered immediately, and he couldn't help the lick of desire that tightened his stomach at the sight of her. She wore a light pink flowered dress that clung to her breasts and fell to just below her knees, showcasing her shapely bare legs. The pink of the dress complemented her cascade of dark hair and the glittering depths of her big brown eyes. She looked utterly beautiful and sexy. She offered him a huge smile that only increased his intense attraction to her.

"Ready to go?" he asked.

She released a musical burst of laughter. "I've been ready for the last hour."

"The only thing you need to remember is to stay close to me and do whatever I tell you to do."

"That won't be a problem," she replied as she grabbed his arm with a teasing smile.

She had the intoxicating scent of exotic fresh flowers, and once again a small flame lit inside him. As they walked away from the shanty, he kept her close to his side as his gaze shot left and right, seeking any potential trouble.

They reached his car, and he was grateful to get a little distance from her as she climbed into the passenger seat and he slid behind the wheel.

"I have to admit, it feels nice to be out of the shanty for a little while," she said as he headed toward town.

"Did you go out a lot before this all happened?" he asked.

"Ella and I would go out at least once a week for shopping or lunch or to get ice cream at Bella's Ice Cream," she replied. "But it isn't just about going out, it's also about nobody being able to come in to visit with me. Layla and Liam Guerin would often pop in for a visit, as did Jaxon and Levi."

"I'm sorry you're missing your friends," he replied sympathetically. "In fact, I'm sorry you're missing your normal life."

"It's okay. Eventually, I'll get my normal life back, and in the meantime, I really appreciate you taking me out today. I promise afterward I'll go back to being a good little prisoner in my own home."

He flashed her a quick glance. "I hate that you have to be a prisoner. I really hate that you have to go through all this, Colette."

She smiled. "It is what it is, right? I'd much rather be a prisoner in my own home than dead. I'm just thankful for getting out for a little while today."

"All you need to remember is if I tell you to do something, no matter how crazy it sounds, just do it without question," he said as he turned into the café's parking lot. "This should go without incident. As long as we're out in public, I can't imagine anyone coming after you."

He pulled into an empty space and parked. "Sit tight, and I'll come around to your door," he said.

Minutes later, the two of them entered the café. The scents of fried fish, hamburger and onions and different simmering vegetables mingled with the yeasty fragrance of freshly baked bread and the sweet smell of cakes and pies.

Crystal Cove Café was owned by Antoinette Le-Blanc, a woman from the swamp. She had bought the café years ago and now lived in a room in the back of the business. It was decorated for home comfort with antique cooking tools hanging from the walls and a large copper fork and spoon that took up nearly one full wall.

It was always busy, but thankfully Etienne found an empty booth toward the back. He guided Colette toward it, and as they passed most of the other diners, several called out a pleasant greeting to her.

Etienne motioned her into the booth seat facing the

back wall while he sat facing the diners where he could see who might approach them.

Colette's friend Ella headed toward them, an order pad in her hand and a wide smile curving her lips. "Colette, it's so good to see you out. I've missed you."

"I've missed you, too," Colette replied with a wide smile. "When this is all over, we'll make plans to go to Bella's and get ice cream."

"I'll be ready whenever you are. How are things going? Have any of your memories returned yet?" Ella asked.

The smile instantly fell from Colette's lips. "Unfortunately, no... Nothing yet."

"Well, it will all work out fine," Ella said with an encouraging smile. "Now, what can I get for you two to eat?"

Colette ordered the shrimp platter, and Etienne got a big burger with onion rings. While they waited for their food to be delivered, they talked about the work she'd gotten done over the last couple of days.

"I finally got my nerve up, and this morning I submitted two articles to the magazines I used to sell to," she replied.

"That's great, Colette. Congratulations on that," he replied. "So how long before you know if they'll buy them?"

"It could be days or weeks or even months. But it felt good to actually submit something after all this time."

Her eyes sparkled brightly as she spoke about her work. They were beautiful long-lashed eyes Etienne could easily fall into. His head filled with the memory of the kiss they had shared, and he tried to push it out of his head.

He tensed as he saw Brett Mayfield and his friend Adam Soreson approaching their booth. He'd heard through the grapevine that both men were pushing hard for the recall.

"Hi, Chief... Colette," Brett greeted them.

"How are you doing, Colette?" Adam asked. He was a big man with wide shoulders. Rumor had it he was one of the best gator hunters around.

"I'm doing just fine," she replied.

"What about you, Chief? You getting any closer to finding the Swamp Soul Stealer?" Brett asked.

"We're working hard to identify him," Etienne said.

"You still got that amnesia stuff?" Adam asked Colette.

"Unfortunately, yes," she replied.

"But that doesn't mean my team isn't working hard to solve these cases," Etienne said. "In fact, we already have several suspects in mind." It was a little white lie, but he couldn't help himself.

"Colette, if you could just remember some stuff, maybe the chief could make an arrest," Brett said. "Everybody in town is waiting anxiously for that to happen."

"I'm trying my very best," she replied, obviously stressed by the conversation.

"If there's nothing else, gentlemen," Etienne said in an obvious dismissal of the two.

Thankfully at that moment Ella appeared with their food, and the two men returned to their seats. However, they weren't the only ones who stopped by their booth.

Angel Marchant and Nathan Merrick said hello to Colette and wished her well as did Shelby Santori, another woman from the swamp. For the most part, the people who stopped by their booth were friendly and offered their support to Colette.

However, besides Brett and Adam, there were a few other men who were less than friendly as they questioned Colette about her missing memories. Etienne took note of everyone who stopped by to talk to her.

Finally, the trail of people stopped, and they were able to eat their meal in relative peace. "I didn't realize I'd be so popular," Colette said between bites.

"You're the woman of the hour," Etienne replied with a grin. The last thing he wanted was for her time away from her shanty to be stressful or unpleasant. "It's the first time people have seen you out and about since your kidnapping so many months ago."

"It was nice to meet Angel's Nathan," she said.

"Do you know Angel well?"

"Not really. We're friendly when we run into each other, but we've never really socialized. Dr. Maison told me what happened to her when I was in the hospital and he was catching me up on recent events." She picked up one of the fried shrimp from her plate and popped it into her mouth... That mouth that taunted and teased him with the desire to cover it with his own.

Damn, what was wrong with him? Never before had a woman affected him in this way. The bad thing was he suspected that if he kissed her again, she would welcome it. If he kissed her again, then he would never want to stop.

"This has been nice," she said once they were finished eating.

"Do you want some dessert?" he asked.

"No, thank you. I'm so full of shrimp I can't eat anything else. But if you want some, go ahead."

He smiled. "I'm so full of burger I can't eat anything else." He gestured to Ella for their check.

"How about we go Dutch on lunch?" she suggested.

"I invited you out. I pay, and I don't want any argument about it," he replied firmly. He paid the tab, and they left for the grocery store.

When they arrived, the store's small lot was filled with cars and trucks. He finally found an empty space near the back and close to the dumpster.

"I don't need too many things," she said.

"Get whatever you need." He shut off the engine, got out and then went around to the passenger door to let her out. Before opening the door, he looked all around the lot, but there was nothing there to give him pause.

"It looks like everyone is shopping today," she said as they walked to the front door.

He kept her close to his side as his gaze continued to shoot around the area.

They entered the store, and she grabbed one of the shopping carts. "What sounds good for dinner tonight?" she asked as they started walking down the produce aisle.

"Whatever you want to cook," he replied. He watched as she put a head of lettuce, a couple of green peppers and an eggplant into the cart.

Several people stopped to say hello to Colette while

others simply stared at her with open interest. She remained composed, offering friendly smiles to everyone. Once again, Etienne couldn't help but admire her inner strength.

He continued to stay close to her, looking for any danger that might come their way. But he saw nobody suspicious.

She moved fairly quicky through the aisles, adding items to her cart as Etienne walked beside her. They got to the meat section where she picked up hamburger and pork chops, round steak and other items he knew she would make for his dinner.

Finally, she was finished, and they headed to the cashier where he insisted on paying the tab.

"You didn't have to do that," she chided as they left the store.

"It's only fair I pay for the groceries since you cook for me every night," he replied firmly.

"Still, it wasn't necessary," she replied.

They left the building and headed for the car. She pushed the cart just ahead of him, and before he could tell her to slow down and walk with him, a sharp crack sounded.

A gunshot.

Colette instantly hit the ground. Oh God, had she been shot?

Etienne grabbed his gun, hunkering down close to the pavement. His heart beat wildly as he looked around, seeking the gunman. Another shot went off, and Etienne identified where the shooter must be. Between two parked cars.

A young couple left the store just then and started to walk into the parking lot.

"Stay back," Etienne yelled at them. "Active shooter!" The last thing he wanted was for any innocent shoppers to get hurt. In fact, he was afraid to return fire, concerned about hitting somebody he didn't want to.

His main concern at the moment was Colette. She was on her back and hadn't moved at all since the first shot.

He grabbed his radio from his utility belt and called for help, then he began crawling toward Colette. His heart beat a dull, sickening rhythm. Was she dead? Had the first bullet struck her? Oh God, that couldn't be. He was supposed to protect her. Why hadn't he sensed the danger lurking in the parking lot? Why hadn't he been more careful?

He finally reached her. He'd been foolish to allow her to leave the shanty.

"Colette?" he whispered to her, his heart already uneven with grief.

Her eyes were closed, and he feared the worst.

"I'm okay," she replied breathlessly and opened her eyes. "He didn't hit me."

A deep relief whooshed through him. He immediately covered her body with his. "We need to stay down until help arrives," he said.

"Okay," she replied and closed her eyes once again.

Etienne remained tense with his gun drawn and pointed in the direction of the shooter. He could feel the frightened tremors that shook Colette's body.

Despite his focus on trying to keep them safe, he

couldn't help but notice the softness and warmth of her body beneath his. He was all too aware of the press of her breasts against his chest and her breath warming the hollow of his throat.

Several times he shouted to stop shoppers from coming into the parking lot. Seconds turned into minutes as he remained covering Colette's body, anticipating another gunshot.

"Chief!" Officers Michael Tempe and J.T. Caldwell finally appeared, guns drawn. Slowly, they approached the area where the gunshots had come from.

Etienne rose to his feet, certain the shooter was gone by now. He grabbed Colette's hand and pulled her up, then hurried her to his car where she slid into the passenger seat.

Michael and J.T. met him at his car, where Officer Joel Smith also joined them. Etienne quickly explained what happened, and Michael went back to the area where the shooter had been to search for evidence. J.T. and Joel loaded the groceries that were still in the cart into the trunk of the car.

All Etienne wanted to do now was get Colette back to her shanty as quickly as possible.

It had been so foolish for him to take her out today. He'd made the decision on an emotional level in an effort to make her happy. He should have kept emotions out of it and made her stay put in the shanty where he knew she was safe.

There would be no more outings. They had gotten lucky today, and she hadn't been physically harmed.

They might not be so lucky the next time. Therefore there would be no more next time.

He'd believed she was in danger from the Swamp Soul Stealer, and today merely confirmed that fact. Obviously, the man was desperate to make sure she died before she could retrieve her memories.

HE DROVE AWAY from the grocery store, livid that his bullets had missed her. It had been the perfect opportunity to take her out. He couldn't believe his luck when he saw her out of her shanty and at the grocery store. It was a moment of vulnerability he'd hoped to take advantage of, and he'd missed the damn mark.

He slammed his fist into his truck's dashboard. Dammit, he had to kill her before she remembered where she'd been and who had held her.

If people found out what he'd done and why, they would never understand it all, even though he thought it made perfect sense. His head filled with a vision of his mother, lying in bed as she cried day after day over his father's long-standing affair.

His father had spent years having an affair with a swamp bitch named Sonya, and he had watched as his mother, Cara, became a shadow of herself. She had refused to divorce his father, but instead lived in a world of grief and humiliation over her husband's long affair.

"Those people from the swamp have work ethics better than you, boy," his father would say to him. "They're stronger and better than you and your snot-nosed friends."

The words whirled around and around in his head.

All he'd ever wanted was his father's love and support, but his father was enchanted with the damn swamp people.

So, his captives were experiments. He was testing them to see just how strong they were. And the truth of the matter was he hated all of them, but he especially hated the beautiful Colette who looked so much like Sonya had when his father's affair first started. It felt good when he beat her. If he could, he'd blow up the entire swamp and all the people in it.

But for now, he just needed one woman dead. He punched his dashboard once again as he thought about his failed attempt moments before.

One way or another, he was going to get to her. And sooner rather than later. Her memories could return at any moment, and then he would be screwed.

He'd blown it today, but there was no way he'd miss the next time. She was a dead woman walking, and in a very short period of time she would just be a dead woman.

COLETTE SAT IN the car and fought against the frightened shivers that still raced up and down her spine. She had heard the first bullet whiz by within inches of her head. It had been sheer terror that dropped her to the pavement.

Some of the terror had now dissipated, but she still couldn't believe that somebody had tried to shoot her... that somebody had truly tried to kill her.

It wasn't any random somebody. It was the Swamp Soul Stealer. God, he'd been in the parking lot with them. Etienne wanted her memories, and the Swamp Soul Stealer wanted her dead before she could give them to him.

She looked out the window where two more officers had joined the others. Etienne was speaking to them all, obviously giving them instructions.

An ambulance pulled up, and Etienne insisted she be checked out by the EMTs. Thankfully, her only injuries were a bruised knee and a skinned elbow, something that must have happened in her fall to the pavement. Etienne insisted he was all right and didn't need to be seen.

It wasn't long after that when he got into the car and turned to her with somber eyes. "Are you doing okay?"

Tears misted her vision, and she quickly swiped at them. She hesitated a moment and then nodded. "I'm okay. I'll tell you one thing…it's going to be a very long time before I'll want to leave my shanty again." Her voice was shaky, and more tears filled her eyes.

"I'm sorry, Colette. I'm so damn sorry about all this. I should have never taken you out and about knowing you were in danger," he said regretfully.

"Please don't apologize, Etienne. I encouraged you to let me go out. I wanted to go out. At least the bullets missed me."

He started the car and pulled out of the parking area, his gaze divided between the front window and his rearview mirror. He reached his hand over and clasped hers. "Thank God you're okay. When I saw you hit the ground, I thought… I thought…" His voice trailed off, and his hand squeezed hers tightly.

She returned the squeeze and once again fought off tears that filled her eyes. He pulled his hand back, and she blinked several times in an effort to rid herself of her tears. "At least we're both okay," she said.

"Thank God for that," he replied.

"Things could have gone much worse," she added.

Neither of them spoke anymore as he continued to drive toward the swamp. Colette still fought off tears of residual fear, but by the time he parked in front of the swamp's entrance, she had managed to get herself under control. Etienne got the groceries from the trunk, and together they headed for her shanty.

Officer Grier rose from the rocking chair as they reached her place. "It's good to see you two okay," he said, a worried frown etching his forehead. "I heard some radio chatter that had me very concerned for you."

"Yeah, somebody took a couple of shots at us in the grocery store parking lot. Thankfully, the bullets didn't hit us, so here we are," Etienne explained. "I'll see you later when I come on duty." He opened the door and ushered Colette inside.

She followed him into the kitchen where he set the grocery bags on the table.

"Are you sure you're okay?" he asked, his beautiful gray eyes concerned as he gazed at her.

"I'm fine. I'm just glad to be back here," she confessed. She felt safe in her shanty. However, as she gazed at the handsome lawman, she realized he looked utterly exhausted. "Etienne, I know you sleep during the afternoons so you'll be awake for your overnight duty here. It's gotten late in the afternoon, and if you want, you can just crash here in my bedroom for a nap rather than driving all the way back to your house," she offered.

He frowned and looked at his watch. "I might just take you up on that."

"I'll make sure it's quiet," she added. Even though she felt safe now, she would feel even more safe if he was here. Besides, if he drove home, it would take even longer for him to get some sleep. "My bedroom is ready whenever you are."

"Are you sure you don't mind?" he asked.

"I don't mind at all," she replied.

He stood and she took him by the hand and led him into her bedroom. She would have preferred to be leading him into her bedroom for something other than him napping, but there was no question that he appeared exhausted.

"Thanks for letting me crash here," he said as he removed his utility belt and gun and placed them on the nightstand.

"It's no problem," she replied easily. "I'm just going to grab a change of clothes. Crawling around on parking lot pavement isn't great for dresses."

She opened a dresser drawer and grabbed a pair of jeans and then went to her closet and pulled a red blouse from a hanger. "I hope you get some good sleep," she said and then pulled the door closed behind her.

She went into the kitchen where she quickly changed out of her dirty dress and into the jeans and blouse.

Once she had put away the groceries, she sank down onto the sofa and released a deep sigh.

It had been a harrowing afternoon. When the first bullet whizzed by her, she'd fallen to the pavement in hopes it would make it more difficult for the shooter to hit her. She had been absolutely terrified, not only for herself, but for Etienne as well. The bullets could have killed him just like they could have killed her. She had never, ever been so frightened in her life.

Thank God they had both survived the attack. She was comforted by the fact he was now sleeping peacefully in her bed.

She got up and went to the back porch to start her generator. She would write for the rest of the afternoon. It would be soothing and would hopefully take the bad taste from the unexpected attack out of her mouth. She had another appointment with Dr. Kingston the next day, and the therapist would probably be able to help her process everything that had happened.

She tried to write, but instead found herself distracted by thoughts of Etienne. She could imagine herself in the bed with him, cuddled up by his side after a bout of lovemaking. The very idea filled her with a heat of desire.

Did he feel the same fire of desire for her? There were moments when she believed he did, when she thought she saw a naked hunger for her shining in the depths of his eyes.

She worked until 5:30 p.m., then closed her laptop and went into the kitchen to see what she was going to make for dinner. She settled on smothered steak and

mashed potatoes. She had just begun to gather the in-
gredients when Etienne came in.

His hair was slightly mussed, and he looked less tired
than when he'd gone into the bedroom.

"Did you get some sleep?" she asked and gestured
him toward the table.

He lowered himself into a chair and smiled. "Actually, I slept better than I have in months. The sounds
of the swamp are very soothing."

"Yes, they are," she agreed and sat in the chair next
to his. "How does smothered steak sound for dinner?"

"Sounds good." He paused for a long moment, his
gaze locked with hers. "You are an absolutely amazing woman, Colette."

She looked at him in surprise as the warmth of a
blush filled her cheeks. "Thank you, but I don't know
what's so amazing about me."

"For one thing, you nearly took a bullet earlier today,
and now here you are calmly talking about what's for
dinner as if nothing at all happened," he replied.

"Oh, trust me, I was terrified this afternoon, but
thankfully it's over, and life goes on," she said.

His eyes were filled with admiration. "Most women
would have crumbled and been afraid for at least the
rest of the day. You are an amazingly strong woman,
Colette."

"I wasn't so strong when I was in that cage next to
Luka." The memory sprang to her mind unbidden, and
her gaze shifted to the wall behind Etienne as it continued to unfold. "Everyone was in a small cage. Occasionally he'd come down to feed us a little or to take

us out to beat us." The words tumbled out of her. "He wore a ski mask, but he was a big man who enjoyed hurting us...and especially me." A shiver raced through her and the back of her throat momentarily closed up.

The memory broke, and she focused back on Etienne. "That's all. I still can't tell you who he is," she said in frustration.

He reached out and grasped her hand. "That's okay," he replied. "Maybe now more things will start to come back to you. You said he came down to feed you. So that implies you were underground. Do you remember how it smelled?"

She frowned and closed her eyes as she concentrated. "Dank and earthy."

"Like a cave of some kind or a basement," he asked.

She hesitated and then opened her eyes. "I'm sorry, I don't know. It could be either."

"That's okay," he repeated and squeezed her hand. His eyes were lit with a new excitement.

"But I didn't remember anything to help you catch this guy," she said in dismay.

"You remembered Luka and that you were held underground someplace. Next time you might remember even more," he replied. "Hopefully your memories are going to start returning to you now." He squeezed her hand once again and then released it.

"I hope so," she said. "Now, how about I go ahead and make dinner, and we can eat a little earlier than usual?"

"That works for me. I might as well hang around here rather than go home before my official guard duty begins."

While she began to cook their meal, he remained seated in the kitchen and the two of them small-talked while she worked. It felt right…having him here in the kitchen with her while she cooked for him, especially since the small snippet of memory had shaken her up.

She loved Etienne's company. She loved the sound of his voice. The truth was she was definitely falling in love with him. However, she didn't expect him to love her back. Oh, he might desire her, but ultimately, she was somebody he had to protect until she remembered enough to get the Swamp Soul Stealer arrested. Once that was done, Etienne would be gone from her life.

Even knowing that, she intended to enjoy each and every moment spent together. And if they fell into bed, she would gladly make love with him even knowing they didn't have a future.

Chapter Seven

The smothered steak was delicious, and their conversation remained pleasant and easy. Etienne was amazed by how quickly she'd bounced back after the afternoon's terrible events.

He definitely admired her strength, not just today, but for all she'd been through, and still she remained standing strong. Despite all that she was facing, she had a cheerfulness and a brightness about her that was incredibly appealing.

He was excited by the fact that memories had begun to return to her. While he didn't have what he needed from her yet, he had hope that in the very near future she would remember something that would lead to an arrest. And God, he hoped it happened sooner rather than later.

He'd told her the truth when he said he had slept better here than ever. The mattress had been soft and seemed to envelop him. The bed had smelled of her soft, floral scent, and he'd fallen asleep almost immediately. He now felt fully rested and ready for the night ahead.

Let him come tonight, he thought as he ate dinner.

Let the bastard come for her tonight so Etienne could finally get him under arrest and in jail.

When he remembered her prone on the parking lot pavement, all his stomach muscles tightened, and he felt slightly sick. He would have never forgiven himself if she had been shot. Thank God she had been okay.

As usual, she looked beautiful tonight. The jeans fit her well, and the red blouse enhanced the darkness of her hair and eyes. He wanted to tangle his hands in her rich, dark cascade of hair. He wanted to kiss her again, this time until they were both breathless and mindless. But he tried to push these thoughts away, knowing they were dangerous.

The steak and mashed potatoes tasted great, but he was definitely hungry for something else. He was having more trouble than usual tonight getting his desire for her under control.

"That was delicious," he began when a knock pulled them both up from the table. "I'll answer it," he said. He drew his gun and opened the door. He immediately relaxed as he saw Thomas Grier.

"Whoa, Chief. Don't shoot me. I just wanted you to know that I'm taking off."

"Okay, I've got it from here," Etienne said as he realized it was seven o'clock and time for Thomas to go off duty.

The two men said their goodbyes, and Etienne closed and locked the door. He knew he should just go on to his post outside, but he was reluctant to end the evening with Colette. Instead, he returned to the kitchen where he offered to help clean up dinner. As usual, she insisted he sit and talk to her while she took care of the dishes.

He told her more funny stories about being the law in Crystal Cove. He loved to make her laugh. Her laughter was full-bodied and contagious, and he loved hearing it.

"Have I told you about Harry, the pet pig?" he asked.

"No," she replied. Her dark eyes were filled with mirth as she finished washing the last of the dishes. "Why don't we go sit in the living room and you can tell me all about Harry the pet pig?" she suggested.

They sat on the sofa together, close enough that he could smell her attractive scent and feel the warmth of her body heat.

"Harry was a miniature pig that belonged to an older woman who treated him like a baby. She dressed Harry in clothes and pampered him like crazy," he said. "But Harry didn't want to be her baby, and the pig was constantly escaping from her home."

"Then what would happen?" she asked.

"Then we would get dozens of calls from the hysterical owner to find Harry. So I would put all my deputies to work finding the pig. And Harry knew all kinds of places to hide. The owner would whine and cry and force her neighbors to join in the hunts until it seemed like the whole town was looking for Harry."

"You're making this up," she accused, her eyes glittering with humor.

He laughed. "I swear it's true. For months, Harry had my deputies and half the town running around to find him. Each time we'd find him and return him until the fateful day when we couldn't find him. We looked high and low for Harry, but he wasn't anywhere to be found."

"You never found him?" she asked.

"No, we didn't. But a week later one of Harry's owner's neighbors had a big barbecue for the neighborhood. He served hamburgers and hot dogs and had a large pot of pulled pork."

"Oh no." She winced and then laughed once again. "You think it was Harry?"

"I do. That was the end of the pig, and I think everyone in town who had dealt with Harry and his owner were extremely happy."

"What about Harry's owner? What happened to her?"

"She moved to Black Bayou," he said, mentioning a small town nearby. "And last I heard she got another pet pig."

"At least you and your deputies don't have to worry about searching for a missing pig anymore," she replied with a grin.

His stomach muscles bunched as fresh desire roared through him.

She got up to turn on the lights against the encroaching darkness of the night. She moved with a natural grace from one lamp to another until a cozy glow filled the room. Returning to the sofa, she sat closer to him than before.

"I should probably get outside," he said.

"Oh, don't go yet," she said, her dark eyes pleading with him. "It's still early, and I'm really enjoying talking to you."

"I suppose I can sit for a few more minutes," he replied.

What he really needed to do was gain some distance from her. Her beautiful, long-lashed eyes beguiled him, and her scent dizzied his senses. Her nearness was a definite temptation, and for some reason tonight he felt particularly weak where she was concerned.

"I've told you my story about Harry the pig," he blurted. "Now it's your turn. Got any swamp stories to make me laugh?"

"Now you've put me on the spot," she replied with another small laugh. "Okay, there was a time a bunch of us got together for a little party. Jackson Dupree provided some of his moonshine…" Her eyes widened, and she clapped her hand over her mouth. "I shouldn't have said that."

Etienne released a small dry laugh. "I know Jackson has a still somewhere in the swamp. We've found it a couple of times and torn it down, but he always manages to get another one up and running before my officers can even leave the old one."

She laughed. "He takes great pride in keeping you all guessing on where his latest still is. Anyway, on this particular night, he brought a bunch of his latest brew for all of us to enjoy, and enjoy we did. Well, I didn't drink any of it because I don't drink, but everyone else wound up pretty smashed."

As she continued to tell him about the antics of the people at the party, all he could focus on was the lusciousness of her full lips. His head filled with the memory of the kiss they had shared, and there was nothing more he wanted to do now than repeat it.

She finished her tale, and suddenly their gazes were

locked. The tip of her tongue danced out to moisten her upper lip. She leaned forward in obvious open invitation, and he couldn't help himself.

He placed his hand on the back of her head, pulled her closer and took her lips with his. Her lips were pillowy soft and so incredibly hot, and her mouth opened up to him. He deepened the kiss, sweeping his tongue over hers.

She leaned even closer and wrapped her arms around his neck. Her breasts pressed against his chest, and all he could think about was how much he wanted her. He felt as if he'd wanted her for months…for years.

The kiss continued until they were both breathless, and he was half-mindless. Her eyes were lit with flames that threatened to consume him.

"Etienne, make love to me." Her voice was slightly husky as she gazed at him. "Come into the bedroom and please make love with me."

"I… We…" He tried to find the words to get things back under control, but control was the last thing he was feeling.

"You know you want to, and I want you to," she continued. "Please, Etienne…give me this one night with you." She grabbed his hand and stood, her dark eyes simmering pools of desire.

He should stop this. He should get up and head directly outside where he belonged.

But that wasn't what he wanted to do. He wanted to take her up on her bold invitation, and when he stood, instead of going straight outside, he allowed her to lead him into the bedroom. Even knowing it was the wrong thing to do, he was absolutely powerless against his desire for Colette.

COLETTE'S HEART THUNDERED in her chest as she led Etienne into her bedroom. Never had she wanted a man as much as she wanted him in this moment. Never had she been so daring with a man as to ask for what she wanted.

His kiss had stirred her to a level she didn't remember ever feeling before. She was on fire with her desire for the lawman...for Etienne. As soon as they stepped into the bedroom, he wrapped her in his arms for another searing kiss.

His hands moved up and down her back, and she was so close to him she could feel his arousal. It only increased her desire for him.

Breaking off the kiss, she moved to the nightstand and turned on a light that gave a soft glow to the room. She watched as he took off his utility belt and placed it on the nightstand.

Stepping closer to him, she unfastened the buttons on his shirt one by one. He stood perfectly still until she was done. Then he shrugged the shirt off his shoulders, and it dropped to the floor behind him.

She released a deep breath as she saw the magnificence of his bare chest. His washboard abs led up to a firmly muscled chest and shoulders that nearly took her breath away. He was so sculpted and beautiful.

He moved closer to her and worked the buttons on her blouse, his touch firing heat through her from head to toe. She let her blouse fall off her shoulders, leaving her in her jeans and a pale pink bra.

He reached for her again and pulled her against his chest as his lips found hers. His naked skin felt wonderful against hers, and her blood heated even more as his fingers worked behind her to unfasten her bra. It fell away, making their skin-to-skin contact even more intimate.

"Colette," he whispered into her ear. "I've never wanted a woman like I want you."

"I feel the same way about you," she replied breathlessly.

He rained kisses across her jawline and then slowly down her neck. She leaned her head back to give him full access to her throat. Each of his nipping kisses fed the fire inside her, a roaring inferno burning eager and hot.

They broke apart, and she removed her jeans while he took off his blue slacks. Him in his black boxers and her only in a wispy pair of light pink panties, they slid beneath the sheets and their lips found each other's once again.

His tongue danced with hers as his hands stroked up her body to cup her breasts.

She moaned with pleasure as his fingers captured one of her nipples and toyed with it until it was peaked with her desire. Then his mouth left hers and slid down to lick and kiss first one nipple, then the other. Electric currents shot from her breasts to the very center of her.

One of his hands slid from her breast and down her stomach. She caught her breath as he reached the waistband of her panties.

At the same time, she stroked across his chest and down his stomach. His skin was warm and felt so good, and he smelled of his wonderful cologne and clean male. He moaned as she caressed farther down until she was at his boxers. She wanted them off. She wanted his complete nakedness next to hers.

She pushed them off him, and in turn he slid her panties down her legs. They came together for another scorching kiss as they writhed against each other. Her naked skin positively loved his.

Once again, he stroked down her body... Slowly, until his fingers reached her most intimate place. She gasped with pleasure as tension began to build inside her. Faster and faster his fingers danced against her moist heat, and the tension inside her reached a peak. She cried out his name as her climax shuddered through her.

Not even waiting to come down from her own pleasure, she took his erection in her hand. Soft, velvety skin covered a hardness that pulsed with an energy that excited her. Despite her climax, she wanted more from him. She slowly moved her hand up and down the hard shaft, and he moaned in obvious pleasure.

He allowed her to caress him for only a couple of moments before he pushed her hand away and rolled her on her back. He knelt between her thighs, and his eyes glittered with a deep hunger as he hovered above her.

"Yes," she whispered urgently, and he slowly entered her.

Another moan escaped her as he filled her completely. He paused for a long moment, his gaze holding hers in a connection that took her breath away with the intimacy of what they were doing.

Slow at first, he moved against her in long, deep strokes. She moved her hips upward to meet him thrust for thrust.

She was lost in him, and as he quickened his strokes, a new rising tension filled her. She clung to his shoulders as he moved faster and faster, taking her to new heights of pleasure.

Then she was there again with another climax exploding inside her. As her body shuddered against his, he found his own release.

Afterward, he leaned down and kissed her with a tenderness that spoke to her very soul. He collapsed just to the side of her, both of them speechless as they each tried to catch their breath. After a couple minutes, he propped himself up on one elbow and gazed down at her.

She could tell by his expression he was about to denounce what they had just shared.

"Don't," she said and reached up to place two of her fingers against his mouth. "Don't you dare tell me that this was all a big mistake."

His lips moved into a grin, and she dropped her hand back to the bed. "Was it that obvious that's what I was going to do?"

"It was obvious enough," she replied. "And it wasn't a mistake. Etienne, if you're honest with yourself, you'll admit that you've been carrying around a lot of desire for me. And I have felt a lot of desire for you. Tonight, we decided to act on that. We're two consenting adults with no significant others, so how can what we just shared be wrong?"

"Well, when you put it that way... I just don't want us to forget what we're here for." He reached out and gently brushed a strand of her hair off the side of her face.

"Etienne, if you're worried about me expecting something from you, then don't. I'm very much aware of what the ultimate goal is."

"As long as we're both on the same page."

"We are," she replied, even though her heart hurt more than a little bit. It was apparent that he didn't feel the same way as she did about their new intimacy. "But I've got to say, I found your lovemaking beyond wonderful, Etienne."

"Same," he replied, his eyes glowing soft in the lamp's light.

She sensed him ready to get up, and she didn't want him to go. She reached up and cupped the side of his face where she could feel the slight stubble of whiskers. "Sleep with me tonight, Etienne. Stay here in my bed for the night. You'll still be on guard duty whether you're outside or in here with me."

He hesitated a long moment and then nodded. "Okay, I'll sleep here tonight."

She smiled as a wave of happiness danced through her. She dropped her hand from his face. "If you want, you can use the bathroom first."

He rolled away from her and got out of the bed. He grabbed his boxers from the floor and left the room.

She released a deep sigh. Their conversation had

definitely been disappointing. There had been a roman-
tic, fanciful part of her that hoped he would confess he
was falling in love with her. Instead, the conversation
was a reminder that once she regained her memories
and the swamp monster was in jail, Etienne would be
gone from her life.

Even knowing this, she couldn't stop herself from
wanting him. She couldn't help that she enjoyed their
conversations and how she looked forward to seeing
him each day.

She definitely couldn't help the fact that she had
fallen in love with him…and she definitely couldn't
help that he didn't love her back.

Even knowing that, she had no intention of guarding her heart. She'd lost six long months of her life,
and now she wanted to live it to the fullest. She'd love
Etienne until he was gone, and then she'd pick up the
pieces of her broken heart.

When he was finished in the bathroom, she grabbed
one of her nightshirts and took her turn getting ready
for bed. Within minutes, she was back in bed with him,
the lamp on the nightstand turned off.

He pulled her into his arms and spooned her with
his arm around her waist. She snuggled into him, loving the feel of his solid body against hers. His breaths
were a warm whisper against her ear, and she'd never
felt so safe and protected.

"Good night, Colette," he said softly.

"Night, Etienne," she replied.

She knew the moment he fell asleep. His breaths became deep and rhythmic. He began to snore softly, the

sound not bothering her at all. Rather it added to the swamp symphony with the bullfrogs croaking and insects clicking and whirring with their nighttime songs.

This felt so right, like this was where they belonged. Yet he'd told her that wasn't the case. Ultimately, she was simply a piece of his puzzle concerning the Swamp Soul Stealer case. He might physically want her, but he didn't love her.

With a deep sigh, she relaxed her body and waited for sleep to overtake her. It was only in her dreams that Etienne the lawman protected her and Etienne the man loved her.

Chapter Eight

Etienne awoke around dawn with Colette still asleep. He was spooned around her warm body as he had been all night, and for a few minutes he simply lay there. Her floral scent surrounded him, and her body heat radiated outward to warm him. It took only minutes of simply enjoying her being in his arms, and then his mind began to race.

Had it been wrong of him to make love to Colette last night? Absolutely. He was in a position of power in their relationship, and as chief of police he should have known better.

Had it been utterly amazing to make love with her? Again, absolutely. She had been giving and so passionate, and her passion had pulled forth a desire in him he'd never felt before. Even now, just being in his arms, she stirred him all over again.

Hell, he hadn't even used birth control. He seriously doubted that she was on pills. He had an old condom in his wallet, but at no time had he thought about putting it on. Things had exploded so quickly between them that protection hadn't even entered his mind. All he could hope was that she hadn't gotten pregnant. That was the very last thing they both needed right now.

It was time for him to get up and get away from her before he repeated his mistake and made love with her all over again. Gently, he pulled his arm from around her, rolled over and slid out of bed.

He moved as quietly as possible, grabbing his utility belt and gun from the nightstand and his uniform from the floor. He crept into the living room, quickly got dressed and went outside to sit in the rocking chair on the porch.

This was where he should have been last night, instead of enjoying the comfort of her bed. This was where he should have been instead of making love with Colette.

Still, what was done was done, and they had to move forward from here. He just didn't want Colette to believe that he was offering her any kind of a relationship when this was all over.

Despite the loneliness he sometimes suffered, he had known for some time that he was destined to live alone. He was married to his job, and there was no room or time for anyone else in his life.

There was no question that he had feelings for Colette... Strong feelings. He loved her laughter and admired her strength. He loved their deep conversations and had an overwhelming desire for her.

However, he didn't know how much of his feelings for her sprang from the fact that she was his star witness. If he didn't need her memories, would he feel the same way about her?

It was evident that she had feelings for him too. But would she feel the same way about him if he wasn't protecting her from a serial kidnapper who wanted her dead? Would she still entertain feelings for him if he wasn't the only person in her life right now?

There were simply too many variables at play to think about any kind of a relationship with her.

Dawn's light painted the swamp with a golden glow, and morning birds called from their perches high in the trees. He was surprised that the Swamp Soul Stealer hadn't made a move on her last night. The rocking chair had been empty all night long, and it probably looked like there wasn't a guard. But the man hadn't shown up.

It was about a half hour later that the generator sounded. Soon after that, the door opened, and Colette smiled at him.

"Good morning," she said, offering him a cup of coffee.

"Thanks," he replied as he took it from her. "And good morning to you."

"How did you sleep?" she asked. She looked beautiful with her long hair slightly tousled and still clad in a light pink nightshirt. It was obvious she had just rolled out of bed and had gone directly to the coffee maker.

"I slept wonderfully well," he replied. It was the truth. With her so warm in his arms, he had fallen asleep almost immediately and slept through the entire night. "What about you?"

"I also slept wonderfully," she replied with a warm

smile. "Well, I guess I'll see you later." With that, she went back inside.

At about ten till eight, J.T. arrived to relieve Etienne. "How you doing, Chief?" the young officer asked.

"I'm doing okay. I see you came prepared for your day of duty." Etienne pointed to the refrigerated bag J.T. carried.

J.T. grinned. "A couple of sandwiches, a couple of sodas, and I'm set for the day."

"Then I'll see you at seven this evening," Etienne replied.

Minutes later, he was in his car and headed to the police station. Later in the day he'd need to go home and take a shower, then try to catch a nap so he could be awake all night. And tonight, he'd be spending his guard duty outside on the rocking chair where he belonged.

He pulled into his parking space behind the station and went in the back door.

Trey met him in the hallway, a frown cutting deep across his forehead.

"What's up?" Etienne asked.

"We've got another one," Trey replied.

Etienne's stomach dropped to the ground. "Who?"

"Kate Dirant's mother just called to report that Kate never made it home last night from a friend's," Trey said.

"Gather everyone, and let's head out there," Etienne replied. He hoped this was just some sort of misunderstanding between mother and daughter. He'd been called out to the Dirant home several times over the past few years when Bettima had called him about young teen Kate running away from home. Kate was now seventeen years old and, according to her mother, just as headstrong as she'd ever been. He hoped this was just another family tiff and not another missing person.

It took twenty minutes before Etienne and Trey were in Etienne's car and heading back to the swamp. Following them were two more patrol cars with four more officers.

"Maybe this time we'll get some clues," Trey said with an optimism Etienne didn't feel.

"That would be nice," Etienne replied. All his muscles were tensed with fiery adrenaline. Along with the adrenaline there was also a deep anger.

Dammit, if Kate had been taken, then who was this person? Why was he doing this? All the questions that had plagued Etienne for the past five and a half months swirled around in his head once again. What the hell was the motive? And where was he keeping his victims?

This one definitely felt personal. It was as if the creep was letting Etienne know that ultimately, he held all the power. Etienne might have Colette, but that didn't stop the perp from taking others at will.

Damn but Etienne wanted this man so badly.

They arrived at the swamp's entrance, and all the officers got out of their cars.

"I know where the Dirant shanty is, so just follow me," Etienne said.

His heart pounded with anxiety as he walked into the swamp to investigate yet another disappearance. God, but he hoped this was just an instance of Kate driving her mother crazy and nothing more ominous. Damn the bastard if he'd taken another one.

Etienne could only hope that this time the swamp monster had gotten sloppy and left something of himself behind.

The men followed him in a silent parade of blue until they reached the Dirant place. Bettima answered on the first knock, her dark eyes filled with tears. "Chief Savoie, she never came home. Kate never came home last night, and I just know she's been taken by the monster. Oh Lord, she's gone, and she's in the grips of the Swamp Soul Stealer."

"Whoa, slow down, and let's take this one step at a time. Where was she supposed to be?" Etienne asked gently.

"At about six last night she went to visit with her friend, Barbie Frasier. Barbie lives just down the way a bit." Bettima wiped away the tears that coursed down her cheeks. "I told her if she was going to go, she should stay the night there. I didn't want her walking home in the dark. I didn't learn until this morning that she left Barbie's about ten last night to come home. But she never got here."

Etienne put his hand on Bettima's plump shoulder. "We're going to look for her now. Can you take me to Barbie's place?"

Bettima nodded, her eyes still brimming with tears. Out on her porch, she pointed to a shanty in the distance. "That's Barbie's place," she said. "It's close, so Kate probably thought she could make it home okay.

Oh, that girl, why didn't she listen to me and just stay the night there?"

As they walked toward the Frasier shanty, Etienne and the officers looked for anything along the path that might be evidence.

They hadn't gone too far when just off the path, Trey found a pink bejeweled cell phone.

"That's Kate's," Bettima said with a deep moan. "Chief Savoie, she would have never just left it here. It was one of her most prized possessions. Oh, she's been taken. She's now one of the vanished."

As the woman began to loudly weep, Etienne motioned to one of his officers. "Bettima, Officer Tempe will take you back to your place, and I'll meet you there in a little while."

Once the two were gone, Etienne turned to his men. "Right around here is where Kate must have been taken. She must have had the cell phone in her hand when she was attacked. So, let's spread out and see if we can find some kind of evidence around here."

For the next two hours, the men searched the area, but they found nothing that might help identify the killer. In truth they found nothing at all. Once again it was like the man was a ghost who took what he wanted and left nothing behind.

They searched all the way to Barbie's place and back to where the phone had been found at least a dozen times. Finally, Etienne called the search off. He instructed two of the officers to conduct interviews with anyone who lived around the area and the rest to go back to the station and resume their normal activities.

He and Trey headed back to Bettima's place to tell the woman the bad news. There was no question in Etienne's mind that the young woman was a victim of the Swamp Soul Stealer.

A half hour later, Etienne and Trey were in Etienne's patrol car and headed back to the station. Etienne had another mother's tears heavy in his heart, staining his very soul.

"Dammit, I wish we would have found something… anything," he finally said in frustration.

"Yeah, me too," Trey replied. "But I don't understand why people in the swamp continue to go out alone after dark knowing they're at risk to be taken?"

"I guess it's human nature to believe it might happen to somebody else, but not to them."

"I figured this creep would be too busy trying to figure out how to get to Colette to be taking any more people," Trey said.

"I'd hoped he wouldn't take anyone else. We definitely can't seem to catch a break in this case." Etienne tightened his grip on the steering wheel, his anger once again rising. "We've gotten nothing from the crime scenes. The guy shoots at us in a parking lot, and we got nothing from that, not even bullet casings. I swear, I want this man so badly I can taste it."

"We all want him, Etienne. We're all doing the best we can to support you," Trey replied.

Etienne shot his right-hand man a quick glance. "I know, and I appreciate the support I get not only from you, but also from all the men and women on the force."

It was true, he had never questioned the support he

got from the people who worked for him. He knew they all had his back, and he was grateful for that.

Back at the station. Etienne went directly into his office to check on other pending issues while he waited for the officers he had left behind in the swamp to check in. As with all the other cases, nobody had seen or heard anything when Kate had been kidnapped. Finally, he headed home, his heart heavy with the day's events.

He showered and pulled on a clean uniform, then fell back in his recliner to catch a quick nap before guard duty that night.

However, sleep remained elusive as the events of the day battled with thoughts of Colette in his mind. He hated the fact that another young woman had disappeared. He needed Colette's memories now more than ever.

What he didn't need was another night like last night. He had to be strong enough to fight the desire that plagued him for Colette. Tonight, he would definitely spend guard duty in the chair outside and not in her bed.

He wound up sleeping for about an hour, and at 6:30 p.m., he left his house to head back to the swamp. His heart was still heavy with the disappearance of Kate. He could only pray that she was still alive, along with the other victims.

He knew this would only feed the recall effort against him. However, he couldn't be bothered by that right now. He knew the mayor was still supporting him, and in any case, more than anything, he wanted—needed—

to be the one to catch this perp. He could only pray that all the victims were still alive.

He pulled into the parking area and left his car. As he walked through the brush and ducked under the Spanish moss hanging from the trees, his thoughts were a jumbled mess.

His anticipation of seeing Colette again mixed with the tragic event of Kate's disappearance.

He hoped like hell the perp came for Colette tonight. While he'd like to shoot the bastard through his black heart, Etienne needed to keep the man alive so he could tell Etienne where all his victims were being held.

As Colette's shanty came into view, Etienne's heart stopped. J.T. was slumped in the rocking chair, and Colette's front door stood wide-open.

He raced across the short bridge to J.T. The officer was alive, but had a nasty head wound. J.T. appeared to·just be regaining consciousness, so Etienne ran into the shanty in a panic.

"Colette," he cried out.

There was no response.

"Colette," he yelled even louder.

She was not in the shanty. His heart dropped, and his knees weakened as the reality of the situation slammed into him. Oh God, the Swamp Soul Stealer had already been here, and he had taken Colette.

COLETTE HAD BEEN in the kitchen finishing up cooking the evening meal when she heard heavy pounding at her front door. She stood in the living room, frozen as her heart beat the rhythm of sudden fear.

The door bowed inward with each heavy blow. With the fourth blow, the lock broke, and the door flew open.

The man of her nightmares stood on the threshold. He was wearing a ski mask, and he wielded a big knife. "I'm going to cut you into little pieces, bitch," he growled in a low, gravelly voice.

With a scream, Colette turned and ran. Without thought, functioning only on fear, she went through the kitchen and ran toward her back door. She threw the door open and rushed outside.

Once out on her deck, she quickly realized she'd run herself into a dead end. Running either way around the deck would only take her back to the front where he could easily catch up with her.

She eyed the murky water below. His rage-filled roar was just behind her. Knowing her very life was on the line, she went over the railing and jumped into the water below.

She gasped as she surfaced, then quickly began to swim toward shore. There were hungry gators and snakes in the water, and there was no way she wanted to be in it a minute longer than she had to be.

As she crawled back up onto land, she looked back toward the shanty. Her attacker was gone. But where? Where was he at this moment?

Terror rose up in her throat. Tears nearly blinded her. What happened to the officer on guard duty? Oh God, had the masked man killed baby-faced J.T.? She didn't want to be responsible for anyone's death.

She had just gotten to her feet when the crashing of the brush behind her let her know the man was still coming after her. She ran—blindly, wildly—through the swamp, her heart threatening to beat right out of her chest. She ran, her progress hampered by the swamp she loved. Spanish moss obscured her vision, and tree roots tried to trip her up.

Despite her best efforts, the man was gaining on her. The darkness of night had begun to fall as she left the narrow path and plunged into tangled limbs and thick brush. Here the darkness was more profound, and as she jumped into a thicket of bushes, she crouched down to hide. She clapped a hand over her mouth to staunch her frantic, terrified cries.

She drew in a deep breath as she heard him coming closer and closer to where she hid. She held completely still, knowing a single twitch or an inadvertent shudder might give away her location.

He came so close to where she hid that she could hear his ragged breathing, imagined she could smell the acrid scent of his sweat. Oh God…so close he came, and then he veered off on another path.

She released a deep sigh of relief, but remained in place, her heart still racing with frantic beats.

And then she heard it… Etienne's voice calling her name.

It came from her shanty and filled her with a new rush of adrenaline. She slowly rose to her feet, the need to be with Etienne searing through her soul. There was safety with him. All she had to do was get back to him and the shanty.

She moved as silently as possible back toward her home. She listened for signs that the attacker heard her... Could he be following her with the intention to kill her before she reached safety?

Tears of fear chased each other down her cheeks as she crept through the tangled vegetation. She stifled a scream as an animal rustled the brush next to her. Where was her attacker now? Was he on a trail walking away from her, or was he silently sneaking up behind her? Finally, her shanty was in sight, and she broke into a full run, her breath escaping her in frantic sobs.

Etienne stood next to J.T., who was seated in the rocking chair with blood running down his face.

"Etienne," she cried as she raced across the bridge.

"Colette!" He drew his gun and opened an arm for her. She finally reached him, and his arm closed around her as he pulled her against his side.

Safe... She was finally safe. The heat from his body warmed the icy chills that filled her. His scent surrounded her like a veil of protection, and her tears were now ones of intense relief.

"I thought you were gone," he said, his voice deeper than usual. "I thought he had taken you again." He squeezed and then released her, his gun still in hand. "Are you okay?"

"I am now." She wrapped her arms around herself and looked with concern at J.T. "Is he all right?"

J.T. offered her a faint smile. "I am now."

"I'm just waiting for some officers to join us here and for the ambulance to arrive to get J.T. to the hospital," Etienne explained.

"I don't need to go to the hospital," J.T. scoffed.

"J.T., you took a hard blow to the head. It was hard

enough to render you unconscious and bloody. You're definitely going to the hospital," Etienne said firmly.

"Chief, he came out of nowhere. I didn't see or hear him until he was on top of me. I don't know what he hit me with, but the blow instantly knocked me out." J.T. released a ragged sigh. "I'm so sorry, Colette. I let you down, and I'm only grateful that you're okay despite my failed guard duty."

"Oh, J.T., please don't apologize. I'm so sorry that you got hurt," Colette replied.

By that time, several other officers had arrived on scene, along with a paramedic who led J.T. off the porch and away from the shanty.

Once he was gone, Etienne gestured Colette and the other three officers into the shanty. He checked the bedroom, the closet and bathroom to make sure the perp hadn't somehow circled back and was hiding somewhere in the place. Once the space was secured, Colette went into the bedroom and changed out of her wet clothes, towel-drying her hair as best as possible.

Back in the living room, she let Etienne lead her to the sofa. He sat next to her while Officers Michael Tempe, Trey Norton and Thomas Grier stood by the front door, ready for whatever he needed from them.

"Now, tell me exactly what happened?" Etienne asked, his eyes the color of cold steel.

"I was in the kitchen when I heard a loud banging on the door." She told him about the door springing open and seeing the man wearing a ski mask and wielding a large knife. She recounted jumping into the water and swimming to shore where the man found her again.

Tears once again fell down her cheeks. "I… I was so sure h-he was going to find me. H-he told me he was going to slice me up, and I knew if he found me, I'd die a horrible death."

"You heard his voice?" Etienne leaned toward her, obviously excited by this news. "What did he say to you?"

"He told me he was going to cut me up into little pieces." She shivered with the horrible memory of that moment.

"Would you be able to identify his voice if you heard it again?"

She hesitated a long moment and then slowly shook her head negatively. "I… I don't know. I don't think so. It was more of a growl. I don't think it was his normal voice."

"Okay." Etienne stood from the sofa. "Let's search to the back door and then outside to see if we can pick up the area where she came out of the water. Thomas, you stay here with Colette."

Minutes later, she was alone with Thomas. She'd known him before her kidnapping, and she used the time with him to catch up on his life and to try to forget what she'd just been through.

"Susie and I got married a month ago," Thomas said.

Colette knew Thomas had been dating Susie Lansbury for a couple of years. "Oh, that's wonderful. Everyone could see that the two of you belonged together. Are you deliriously happy?"

Thomas laughed. "I am happy. We're already planning our family."

"I'm so happy for you, Thomas." She released a deep

sigh. "That's what I want for myself...true love and a houseful of babies."

And she knew who she wanted that with, but she had a feeling she was wrestling with the wrong gator. All she knew right now was that she was grateful to be alive after the close call she'd just suffered.

She and Thomas continued to chitchat as they waited for the other officers to come back. Residual fear still danced through her veins, and all the while questions whirled in the back of her head.

Would she still be safe here with a guard sitting outside her door? Her front door definitely needed to be fixed before she'd even consider staying here. But even then, would she feel safe?

The Swamp Soul Stealer had nearly gotten to her tonight. What would keep him from doing the same thing on another night? He could sneak up on another guard too. Then he would come inside and...

Surely Etienne would figure out a plan to make sure she wasn't vulnerable here again. She trusted him. After all, she was his star witness once enough of her memories returned to give him an arrest.

It was about an hour later when Etienne and his men came back to the shanty. Their expressions were grim.

"Nothing," Etienne said in disgust. "Once again, this creep has left us with absolutely nothing to go on." He sat next to her and raked a hand through his hair in obvious frustration. He stared at the broken door for several long moments, his eyes still a deep steel gray... hard and focused.

"You can't stay here," he said to her. "It's obviously no longer safe."

"So, where am I going?" she asked curiously.

"Pack some bags," he said tersely. "You're coming home with me."

Chapter Nine

Colette's head reeled as she packed some clothes and toiletries to go to Etienne's house. The entire evening felt like a bad dream. The attack had definitely been something out of her very worst nightmare.

As she thought about the man with the knife, icy chills shot through her body. There was no question that had he caught her, she'd be dead. He would have killed her in a most painful way. He'd almost been successful at getting to her tonight.

Surely, she'd be safe at Etienne's house. He wouldn't be taking her there if he didn't believe that.

She finished packing her things and carried her bag into the living room where Etienne was pacing the floor.

He stopped in his tracks at the sight of her. "Ready?"

"Ready," she replied.

He walked over and took the bag from her. "Go ahead and pack up your laptop too. I'm sure you'll want that while you're at my place."

She quickly packed it up in its padded case, then turned back to Etienne expectantly.

"I'm leaving Thomas here to stand guard until we can get the door fixed," he said.

"I can call Brett Mayfield in the morning. I'll arrange with him to come out and fix it as soon as possible," she replied.

"At least that hotheaded loudmouth is good for something," Etienne growled as the two of them headed for the door.

Outside, Thomas sat in the rocking chair. "Don't worry, Colette," he said. "I'll make sure nobody goes in the house while it's unlocked."

"Thank you, Thomas. I really appreciate it."

"And I'll continue to keep a guard on the place until the door is fixed and the shanty can be locked up," Etienne added.

Minutes later, they were in Etienne's car and headed toward town. He was quiet on the ride and gave off a tense, angry energy. Was he angry because he was taking her to his home? Was he mad that she would now be his full-time burden? When he'd taken her home from the hospital, he certainly hadn't signed up to become a full-time babysitter.

If she had anyplace else to go, she would go there. But she refused to stay with any of her friends and bring this danger to their doorstep. A motel room certainly wouldn't offer any sort of great protection.

Damn her own mind for keeping her memories locked up so tightly. If only she could remember what had happened to her in the three months she'd been with the monster, then Etienne might be able to arrest the man and save the others. If she could just remember, then this would all be over.

Just when despair started to take hold of her, he

reached over and covered her hand with his. "You doing okay?" he asked with a softness that soothed the ragged edges of her current thoughts. He pulled his hand away and placed it back on the steering wheel.

"I'm okay," she said. She hesitated a moment and then continued, "But you seem angry. Are you upset that you have to take me home with you?"

"Not at all," he replied immediately. "But I am angry. I'm mad that this creep attacked my officer and then went after you. I was so scared, Colette." He paused for a moment. "When I went into the shanty and you weren't there, I was certain you'd been killed or taken once again." His voice was deep and filled with myriad emotions.

Maybe he did care about her a little bit. Maybe he cared about her more than just as a piece to his crime puzzle. Perhaps he cared about her simply as a woman.

She sat up straighter in the seat as he pulled into the driveway of an attractive ranch house. In the darkness of the night, it was impossible for her to tell what color it was. With the push of a button on his visor, the garage door opened, and he pulled inside. He grabbed her bag from the back seat, and she reached for her laptop. As the garage door closed, he guided her into the house.

They entered an airy kitchen with a nice black table and four chairs. Turning on lights, he led her through an attractive living room with a black sofa and a matching recliner. A big television was mounted on one wall. A glass-topped coffee table matched the end tables. It all appeared rather cold and sterile, with no photos on the walls and nothing to indicate that Etienne lived here. The house could have belonged to anyone.

From the living room, she followed him down the hallway and into the first room on the right. There, a queen-size bed was covered with a dark blue spread, and matching curtains hung in the single window. A double dresser lined one wall, and nightstands with attractive silver lamps flanked the bed.

"I hope you'll be comfortable here," he said as he placed her bag at the foot of the bed. She set her laptop there as well.

"This is lovely. I'll be just fine here," she replied.

"There are several empty drawers in the dresser, and the bathroom is across the hall. You should find everything you need in the cabinets beneath the sink. Now, since it's so late, we'll just call it a night, and I'll see you in the morning."

"Etienne...thank you for all of this," she said.

He smiled, the smile that always melted something deep inside her very soul. "No problem. I'll just say good night now, and if you need anything at all, I'll be in the living room."

It wasn't until he closed the door behind him that she wondered why he would be in the living room and not in his bedroom. The thought only lasted a moment as she opened her bag and pulled out a nightgown. She would unpack and really settle in tomorrow.

She grabbed her gown, along with her toothbrush and toothpaste, and went across the hall to the bathroom. She found a washcloth under the sink and proceeded to wash her face, brush her teeth and change into the nightgown.

Back in the bedroom, she pulled the curtains more tightly closed over the window. Only then did she fold down the bedspread to expose inviting light blue sheets. Finally, she crawled into the bed and turned off the lamp.

The room was plunged into total darkness. She'd never been afraid of the dark before, but tonight it definitely bothered her.

Where once she had found the dark comforting, she now found it cloying and claustrophobic. This was where the monster lived…in the shadows of the night. This was where the monster played his games of taking people away from their loved ones and into his lair.

The dark had once been a safe place for her, but now she knew it could be a very dangerous place.

As these thoughts whirled around and around in her brain, she reached out and turned on the bedside lamp once again. The soft glow would keep the monsters away.

She finally closed her eyes and fell into a nightmare where she was being chased through the swamp. She tripped over roots and tangled with tree limbs that tried to hold her captive. Spanish moss wrapped around her, further impeding her frantic escape from whatever was chasing her.

She was desperate, her breaths releasing in deep pants as tears blurred her vision. She had to get away before he caught her. She had to… Thick fingers touched the small of her back, and she screamed.

She jerked upright in the bed, her gaze shooting

around the room. Light lit around the edges of the curtains, letting her know it was after dawn.

She released a shuddering sigh and then screamed again as the bedroom door flew open and Etienne entered with his gun drawn.

He took one look around and then holstered his gun. "You okay?" he asked.

She nodded, embarrassed that she must have screamed out loud with her nightmare. "I'm sorry. It…it was a bad dream."

"As long as you're okay, that's all that matters," he replied.

What she wished in that moment was that he would embrace her, maybe stroke her hair or her cheek and tell her he was sorry she'd had a nightmare.

He was already dressed in his blue uniform, and he smelled of minty soap and shaving cream.

"What time is it?" she asked.

"A little after eight. Whenever you're ready, I'll get breakfast going."

"Oh, Etienne, you don't have to cook for me," she protested.

He offered her a small grin. "Are you planning on never eating while you're here?"

"Hmm, let me rethink this," she replied with her own grin.

He laughed. "Whenever you're ready, the coffee is made. I'll be in the kitchen." With that, he left the room.

She got out of bed and grabbed a pair of jeans and a light purple T-shirt from her bag. She got dressed, washed her face and brushed her teeth and hair. By the time she left the bathroom, the nightmare had begun to recede from her thoughts.

After all, was it any wonder she'd had nightmares after the night she had endured?

The smell of fresh-brewed coffee led her to the kitchen where she found Etienne seated at the table and drinking a cup. He jumped up to his feet at the sight of her.

"Here...sit," he said as he pulled out one of the chairs at the table.

She sat while he went to a cabinet, pulled down a cup and poured her coffee. "This feels backward," she said. "Normally, it's me offering you a cup of coffee in the morning."

He set the cup before her and smiled. "Different circumstances call for different actions." He sat back down in the chair opposite her. "Except for your nightmare, how did you sleep?"

She wrapped her fingers around her cup, seeking its warmth as memories of her bad dream rushed through her head again. "I honestly couldn't tell you. Even though I know it's not true, it seemed like I fell into the nightmare immediately."

"Do you want to talk about it?" he asked with a gentleness that washed over her.

"There isn't a lot to tell. I was just running away from something or someone chasing me through the swamp."

"With what you went through last night in real life, it's no wonder you had a nightmare like that." He took a sip of his coffee, then stood. "On the menu this morning is bacon and eggs any way you like them."

"That sounds good to me, and I like my eggs however you want to make them," she replied. "Actually, if you'll show me where things are, I'd be glad to cook."

"This morning you're getting a visitor's welcome, and I'll cook for you," he replied. He pulled a skillet out of one of the lower cabinets and got a pound of bacon from the refrigerator.

"Okay, but I'm offering my cooking skills to you whenever you want them," she said.

"How about I cook our breakfasts, and you can take care of the evening meals?"

"That sounds like a good deal to me," she agreed. She watched as he laid the bacon strips into the skillet. Within minutes, the meat was sizzling, filling the air with its aromatic scent. "So, we now know who is cooking what meal, but what are we doing in between those times?" she asked curiously.

"Unfortunately, you're going to be going to the station with me during the days. Needless to say, you'll be completely safe there. We'll set you up in one of the interview rooms, and you can work there. I know it's not ideal, but it's where we're at right now."

"And it will be just fine," she assured him. "Etienne, the last thing I want is to be an unnecessary burden. Stick me wherever you need to, and I'll be just fine."

He smiled at her. "I appreciate that." He turned back to the skillet and began removing the crispy bacon. "Now, how do you want your eggs?"

"Really, Etienne, I don't care. Whatever is easiest for you," she replied.

"Okay then, scrambled it is."

As he made toast and cooked the eggs, they small-talked about favorite breakfast foods. There was something quite intimate about sitting in the kitchen laughing and talking with a man making the morning meal.

His uniform really fit him well, emphasizing his broad shoulders and slim waist and hips. Just looking at him brought up memories of their lovemaking, something she would love to repeat.

However, it was clear that wouldn't happen, and sadly, she would have to live with that.

It didn't take long before he had breakfast on the table. As they ate, he explained what their schedule would be during the days…noting that it could change at any given moment. "No matter what I'm doing, you'll remain in the interview room where we've set you up," he explained. "I'm sure this creep won't even try to come for you in the police station."

"I agree," she replied. "Surely he wouldn't be that stupid."

"One thing is certain, this man isn't stupid," Etienne replied.

They finished eating, and she helped with the cleanup. He pulled a couple pork chops from his freezer and set them on the counter to thaw. She went back to her bedroom and grabbed her computer case, and they were ready to go.

They left the house through the garage, just as they had entered the night before. As she slid into the passenger seat, he opened the garage door with a touch of a button on his visor.

They both were silent for the rest of the ride to the police station. Once there, he hurried her to the back door, and they walked down a long hallway to a relatively small room. A table for six took up most of the space.

"You can get settled in here," he said.

She put her computer case on the table and smiled. "I'll be just fine here," she replied. "Now, you go do your police work and don't worry about me."

"Then unless something comes up, I'll see you around noon for lunch." With that, he left the room and closed the door behind him.

She took her computer out of the case, plugged it into a nearby wall socket and got set up to work. At least with all this uninterrupted time, she should get a lot of writing done.

Unfortunately, with all the uninterrupted time, she also had plenty of time to think. And her thoughts always went to Etienne.

She couldn't believe how easily he'd won her heart. Was it simply a matter of circumstances? Would she have fallen in love with any man who was protecting her from a potential killer? A man who was her sole connection to the outside world?

No, she didn't think so. She had fallen in love with Etienne the man and not Etienne the lawman. Her love for him sprang from the long conversations and the laughter they shared. It had grown from the intense physical attraction they had for each other and a million other things.

But no matter how much she loved him, she couldn't

make him love her back. His love remained as elusive as the memories locked so tightly in her mind.

ETIENNE SAT IN his office, his thoughts on the woman he had left in the interview room. She could have been so difficult. She could have complained about being stuck in a small room with no television, no sofa, nothing but a table and her laptop for company.

However, one thing he'd learned about Colette was she was definitely not a complainer. Instead, she easily rolled with the punches and remained pleasant under almost all circumstances.

There was no question that he admired her. She was the strongest woman he'd ever met. There was also no question that he wanted her. He'd never felt such wild, sexual attraction for a woman before.

But that didn't mean he was in love with her. He refused to even consider that he might be.

He also doubted that her feelings for him were real. They were in an unusual situation, filled with forced proximity and danger. It was only natural that emotions would run high between them. But those emotions definitely couldn't be trusted.

With a deep sigh, he pulled out the large file he had on the Swamp Soul Stealer kidnappings. It held all the circumstances of the disappearances, all the interviews that had been conducted and any other information pertinent to the investigation. It now contained the interview and information about Kate's kidnapping as well.

He began to read through the file in hopes of spotting something that had been missed. He had read it all a hundred times before, but he kept thinking he was missing something. As he read, he took notes, fully immersing himself in everything having to do with the crimes.

It took him well over an hour to read through everything, but when he was finished, he had another suspect in mind. Pierre Gusman was another one of the gator hunters in the area. He was physically capable of carrying a body through the swamp.

Etienne hadn't paid much attention to the man when he showed up at the scene when Colette had been taken. It wasn't until right now, reading through the file, that he realized Pierre had shown up at all of the crime scenes.

When the police arrived to investigate a disappearance, it always drew a small crowd of onlookers. But Pierre had been there every single time, and there was no reason for him to be. The crimes had occurred all over the swamp.

Etienne knew from his study of criminals that often the guilty party would insinuate himself somehow into the investigation. While Pierre had remained a silent observer, the fact that he was at each scene definitely drew Etienne's attention now.

He pulled out his phone and called Trey. "Come to my office."

"Be right there."

Moments later, Trey sat down in the chair in front of Etienne's desk. "What's up?"

"I've just been going through the file and something caught my attention," Etienne began.

"Oh yeah?" Trey leaned forward.

"As usual, it might mean nothing, or it might mean everything. Have you or any of the men had any run-ins with Pierre Gusman?"

Trey frowned. "No, not that I'm aware of. I've seen him around town, and all I know about him is that he's a quiet man and somewhat of a loner. Why?"

"Did you realize each time we've gone out to investigate a disappearance, he's been around in the group of people we always draw?" Etienne asked.

Trey frowned. "No, I didn't realize that. He's been at every single one of the crime scenes?"

Etienne nodded. "According to the notes where we chronicle who's present at each scene."

Trey's frown deepened. "That's odd. Was anyone else present at all the scenes?"

"No, just Gusman."

"So, is he the Swamp Soul Stealer and checking up on our investigation at each scene? Or is he just an odd man interested in police work and what's going on in the swamp?"

"This is definitely something I'd like to follow up on. Why don't you and Joel go have a conversation with the man and see what kind of a vibe you get from him? Check his alibis for the nights of the disappearances and see if you think he's a viable suspect."

"Got it," Trey said, "I'll grab Joel, and we'll leave as soon as possible. I'll get back to you with what we find out."

Etienne would have liked to be the one going to speak to Pierre, but he felt an odd obligation to stick around the building with Colette here. Besides, he trusted Trey. If there was any information to get, Trey and Joel would get it. It was probably a crapshoot anyway.

Etienne went back to reading the file. He finally stopped when his stomach rumbled with hunger, and he realized it was 12:30 p.m.

He got up and stretched, then headed down the hallway to the interview room. "Did you think I was going to starve you to death?" he asked as he entered.

Colette looked up from her keyboard and laughed. "I figured sooner or later you'd come and take pity on me."

"We have a couple of options for lunch. I can get one of the guys to get us burgers from Big D's, or we can order something from the café, and they'll deliver it here."

"I love Big D's cheeseburgers, so that would be fine with me," she replied.

"Okay, then burgers it is. French fries or onion rings?"

"French fries," she said.

"And what would you like to drink?"

"A regular soda is fine."

He nodded. "Got it. I'll come back when the food arrives."

He left the room that now smelled of her soft floral scent. He asked Michael to run to Big D's for them, then he sat back down at his desk.

Twenty minutes later, Michael was back with the food, and Etienne brought it to Colette in the interview room. "I've got your cheeseburger and fries right here," he said as he took the food out of the paper bag.

"And what did you get?" she asked. She took a straw from him and punched it into the plastic top of her soda.

"A double burger with onion rings and an iced tea to drink," he replied.

They unwrapped their sandwiches and began to eat. They talked about their favorite menu items at Big D's, and the conversation remained light.

It was always like that with her. Their conversations always flowed so effortlessly. Even when they disagreed about something, it still remained easy between them.

"Are you bored to death in here?" he asked.

She popped a french fry into her mouth and chased it down with a quick drink of soda. "No, not at all," she replied. "I finished one article, got it ready for submission and started on a new one. I was just about to take a break and jump on the internet for a little while. As long as I have my computer, I won't get bored. How has your morning been?"

"Fairly quiet. Do you know Pierre Gusman?" he asked and then bit into his burger.

She looked at him in surprise. "Yes, I know Pierre, although not well. Why?"

"His name just came up as I was reading through the kidnapping file. I find it odd that every time we've gone out to investigate one of the disappearances, he's been around the scene."

"He's an odd fellow. He lives in a small shanty near mine, but he keeps to himself. He's not exactly unfriendly, but he doesn't go out of his way to be friendly with anyone either," she said.

This information only made Etienne more interested

in the man. Pierre was somebody who would know the swamp like the back of his hand. He would know places to hide and keep people captive.

But he might just be an odd, innocent man, Etienne reminded himself.

They finished their lunch, and Etienne left her once again. It was about two o'clock when Trey and Joel returned. They immediately came into Etienne's office to share what they'd learned from Gusman.

"He does seem to be an odd duck," Trey said. "His alibis for the kidnappings were all the same. He was in the swamp gator-hunting alone. That was also his alibi for the night Kate went missing."

"He said he was at each scene when we were investigating because he was interested in what was going on in the swamp," Joel said. "He wanted to know if we'd found any clues that would catch the man responsible for the disappearances."

Etienne released a deep sigh. "So, the man might be guilty, or he might not be guilty."

"That's about the size of it," Trey replied. "I will tell you that something about the man gave me the creeps."

"Me too," Joel said.

"Any reason for that?" Etienne asked curiously.

"Nothing I can put my finger on, he just gave me the creeps," Trey said.

"Same," Joel added.

"Tomorrow, maybe I'll take one of the other men and have another conversation with him," Etienne said thoughtfully.

"That's probably a good idea. Maybe if we put a little pressure on him, he'll crack if he's guilty," Trey said.

"We should be so lucky," Etienne replied wryly.

At five o'clock, he went to pick up Colette from the interview room. She packed up her computer, then they left to head to his place. At least with Colette in the police station during the days and staying with him at night, he could return to his normal work routine.

Once they were home, she got busy cooking dinner. He sat at the kitchen table while she worked, telling himself it made sense that he be on hand to help her find things in the kitchen. Along with the pork chops, she was making honey-sweetened carrots and mashed potatoes. He was definitely going to have to get groceries. What with Colette cooking him meals when he was on guard duty at her shanty and him rarely being home at dinnertime at all, his cupboards and refrigerator were pretty bare.

"It's a real treat to have an oven and four burners," she said.

"And just think, you don't have to go outside to take a shower."

The minute the words left his mouth, he was tortured by a vision of her naked body beneath a steamy spray of water. He was in the vision with her, slowly sliding a bar of soap across her shoulders and down her back and across her full breasts.

He shook his head and consciously forced the vision out of his brain. What the hell was he doing to himself? And why was he thinking such inappropriate thoughts about her? All he needed to do was keep her safe and nothing more. It shouldn't be this difficult.

Her voice pulled him from his thoughts. "This is going to take another thirty minutes or so before it's ready."

"That's fine," he replied. He'd like to leave the kitchen for some much-needed distance from her, but he also didn't want to leave her alone in case any trouble appeared.

He had good security around the house with alarms on all the doors and windows. As the chief of police, he'd wanted good security in case some disgruntled criminal came after him. But security systems could be breeched, so he intended to stay ready for anything.

She set the table and then took the chair opposite his. "Before this case sucked up all your time, what did you do to pass the evenings?"

"When the weather was nice, I would walk down to visit with my parents, or I'd just watch television until bedtime."

"I'll bet your favorite shows are the crime dramas," she said.

He laughed. "You'd be wrong. Usually, I watched sitcoms and game shows. The last thing I want to do after a long day of worrying about crime is watch it on television."

"That makes sense," she replied. "So tonight, you can educate me on game shows and sitcoms since I've never watched either."

He nodded. "Sounds like a plan."

What he'd really like to educate her on was how to

retrieve memories that could possibly put the Swamp Soul Stealer in jail. And the sooner, the better.

Because he knew this arrangement of Colette staying here with him was going to be a test of his willpower. It was a test he feared he might fail.

Chapter Ten

For the next five days they fell into an easy routine. Colette spent her days in the small room at the police station. Each day, Etienne ate lunch with her, and around five o'clock, they would come home. She would cook dinner and in the evenings they watched television.

She was grateful that J.T. was back at work after having suffered a concussion. While at the police station, she had also met Officer Annie DeRossit, the only woman on the force. Brett Mayfield had replaced her front door, so her shanty could be locked up and no longer needed a guard on duty there. Colette continued her therapy with Dr. Kingston, but she still hadn't remembered anything more.

It was around 6:30 p.m. when a knock fell on the door. They had just cleaned up the kitchen after dinner. Etienne immediately grabbed his gun and went to check the door.

He looked considerably more relaxed when he returned, ushering in an older couple. He introduced her to Diana and Lester Savoie, his mother and father.

"I hope we aren't interrupting your evening, but

Mama wanted to check in with her baby boy," Lester said with a fond look at Diana.

"You aren't interrupting anything at all," Colette said, smiling warmly.

They were an attractive couple. It was easy to see where Etienne got his curly hair as Lester had salt-and-pepper curls. His mother had chin-length dark hair and gray eyes that matched her son's.

When they were all seated in the living room, Diana offered Colette a smile. "I've been wanting to meet you for a while, Colette. I'm so sorry for everything you've been through. What incredible strength you must have."

Colette returned her smile. "Thank you. And thanks to your son, I'm still here. Still standing."

Lester grinned with obvious affection at his son. "He's a good one."

"Have you heard about the recall effort?" Etienne asked.

"Ack…a bunch of foolishness by a bunch of fools," Diana scoffed.

"I definitely agree," Colette said. "I can certainly attest to how hard Etienne has been working to solve these cases."

"We know how hard he's been working," Lester replied and looked at Etienne. "Are you sleeping any better?"

"Maybe a little bit better," Etienne replied.

"I'm sure he isn't getting enough sleep," Colette replied with a long look at the lawman. She now knew he spent his nights in his recliner chair in the living room. Not a place to get good, restful sleep.

"But I am eating well," Etienne said. "Colette cooks dinner every night, and she's a very good cook."

"Well, that's good," Diana replied. "A mother always wants to know her children are well-fed."

"I'm definitely enjoying the benefits of a kitchen with all the modern bells and whistles," Colette said with a small laugh.

"Do you miss your home in the swamp?" Diana asked.

"Not too much. I'm enjoying your son's company, and that makes it easier to be away from my shanty," Colette replied.

In fact, she'd been surprised by how little she had missed her home. This felt like home...right here with Etienne. Still, eventually she knew she would return to her shanty, probably sporting a very big broken heart.

For the next few minutes, she listened to Etienne and his parents visit. They talked about relatives who didn't live in Crystal Cove and the latest project Lester was working on. Apparently, the man had a wood-carving hobby he was quite good at. He was currently carving a unicorn out of a fallen tree limb.

"It's coming along beautifully," Diana said. "But you know your father... Once he starts on one of his projects, he forgets he has a wife who might need a little attention too."

"Oh, now, Mama, that isn't true. I always have time and attention for you," Lester replied with a wink at his wife.

It was around eight o'clock when they left. "Your parents are absolutely delightful," Colette said as Etienne closed the front door after telling his parents goodbye. "It's obvious they love you very much."

"Yeah, I'm kind of fond of them too," he replied with a grin.

"They also seem to be pretty crazy about each other. How long have they been married?" she asked.

"It will be forty-one years this November," he replied.

"That's amazing. So you've had a really good example to follow when it comes to marriage."

"True, but that doesn't mean marriage is something I want for myself." His gaze didn't quite meet hers.

"Why not, Etienne?" she asked curiously.

He finally looked at her. "I thought I wanted it at one time, but over the past couple of years, I've realized I'm probably better off alone."

"Why would you come to that conclusion?" she pressed, wanting to understand him. If he didn't want a relationship with her, then why shut himself off from any relationship in the future?

"I'm married to this job. There's really no time for anything else in my life," he replied.

"Etienne, once this case is over, you'll be back to regular working hours, and you'll have time for a special woman in your life," she said. Oh, how she wished she could be that special woman for him, but obviously she wasn't.

"Why do you care whether I get married or not?"

A blush warmed her cheeks. "Because I care about you, Etienne, and I just know you would be a great husband to some woman. I'd like you to find a special woman who would love and support you and could be your soft place to fall." Couldn't he see that woman was her? Oh, why couldn't he love her like she loved him? It felt so unfair. After all she had been through, why couldn't fate or whatever grant her this particular wish?

"I appreciate your sentiment," he replied. "And I wish the same for you. I hope you find a special man who will love and support you and be your soft place to fall. And now, it's getting late, so I suggest we head to bed."

She had a feeling it was the topic of conversation that made him ready to call it a night. Half an hour later, Colette slipped beneath the sheets, but she kept the lamp on the bedside table on. She hadn't had any more nightmares and had actually slept peacefully each night. But she kept the light on every single night...to keep the monsters away.

She awakened early the next morning refreshed after another good night's sleep. The scent of coffee let her know that Etienne was already up and around.

She gathered clean clothes and went across the hall where she started the water for a shower. As she stood beneath the warm spray, she admitted that she had been fully seduced by the conveniences a place in town offered.

Cooking meals with the luxury of an oven, a microwave and four burners was terrific. But the real luxury was being able to step into a shower that had hot water and a healthy spray, something she definitely didn't have in her relatively primitive shower on her back porch.

Dressing quickly in a pair of jeans and a maroon

long-sleeved blouse, she pulled her wet hair into a low ponytail, ready to face the day.

"French toast," Etienne said in greeting when she walked into the kitchen.

"Sounds yummy." She grabbed a cup from a cabinet. She poured herself some coffee and then sat at the table.

"You sleep well?" he asked as he turned back to the skillet.

"Like a baby," she replied. "What about you?"

"I slept off and on."

"What time did you get up?" she asked.

"Early enough," he replied vaguely. "I already ordered some groceries, and they arrived a few minutes ago."

So, as usual, he hadn't gotten a good night's sleep. She had no idea how late he stayed up at night, and he was always up before her in the morning. The man was running on an empty tank. The fact that he functioned so well during the day spoke of his inner strength.

He was being eaten alive by the Swamp Soul Stealer case. That must be what kept him from sleeping. As always, guilt filled her heart—she could help him if she just could remember.

"I'm hoping for the morning when I ask you how you slept and you tell me you slept like a baby," she said.

"Ha, I'm hoping for that day too. I've always had a little trouble sleeping, but since these disappearances, it's gotten much worse." He dropped two of the egg-and-milk-covered slices of bread into the pan.

Dammit, if only she could remember something… anything that might help solve the crime. So far, she'd pretty much been deadweight for him, unable to offer anything that might move the case forward.

It wasn't long before the French toast was ready, and they sat down to eat. "I love maple syrup," she said as she poured a liberal dose over her French toast.

"I see that," he replied in amusement. "You just drowned a perfectly good breakfast."

"I didn't drown it," she protested with a laugh. "I just enhanced my breakfast."

"If you're lucky, I'll make you waffles tomorrow morning and you can have a plateful of syrup again."

"That sounds delightful," she said with another laugh.

Once they were finished eating, she helped clean up the kitchen, and they left for the police station.

She stared out the passenger window as he drove, her thoughts as scattered as the leaves knocked down from the trees by the gusty wind blowing outside. While she knew it was necessary for her to be ensconced in the little room in the police station, there was a part of her that wondered how long this arrangement would last.

She knew this was the best way to keep her safe, but spending all day in the room was becoming quite monotonous. How long before this whole ordeal would be over? How long before Etienne became sick of her presence in his home?

Right now, they seemed to still be in a sort of honeymoon phase. She thought he enjoyed spending his evenings with her. Their conversations remained pleasant, and they often laughed together. But eventually she feared the honeymoon would be over. Not for her, but for him. He'd tire of her presence, and then what would happen?

Damn, if only she could just remember something.

She released a deep sigh as he pulled into his parking space at the back of the police station.

He shut off the engine and turned to look at her. "That was a pretty heavy sigh. Is everything all right?" His eyes held a wealth of concern.

"Everything is fine," she assured him.

"Are you sure?"

"I'm positive." She offered him her brightest smile. There was no way she was going to share with him her troubling thoughts, especially since he couldn't say or do anything to solve her worries.

"Okay, hang tight, and I'll be around to get you out." He opened her door and gestured for her to step into the safety of one of his arms.

As always, his close proximity caused her heart to flutter. He smelled of shaving cream, his spicy cologne and a male scent that was his alone. If she was blindfolded and five men stood before her, she was certain she could pick out Etienne by his scent alone.

The minute they stepped into the building, his arm dropped from around her. They walked down the hallway, and she turned into her room and set her computer case on the table.

"Would you like for me to grab you a bottle of water or a cup of coffee?" he asked.

"No, thanks, I'm fine. I'll just see you around noon." She opened her laptop as he murmured a goodbye and left the room.

She set up her computer, plugged it into a nearby outlet and sank down in the chair. There was one thing for certain, with all the uninterrupted time, she was getting a lot of writing done. Not only had she submitted several articles, but she had also restarted her blog. It would take months for her to build up the readers she had once had, but at least she was working on it again.

She turned her computer on and waited for it to load. While she was waiting, a vision slowly unfolded in her mind. She closed her eyes to bring it into clearer focus.

She was chained to a wall in a cage...a concrete wall. She and the others were in a basement. Not some cave or anyplace in the swamp. A basement! That was all the vision showed her, but it was enough.

She jumped up out of her chair, ran to the door and tore it open. She wasn't sure where Etienne was right now, but she had to find him as soon as possible. Somewhere in Crystal Cove there was a basement filled with the missing.

J.T. suddenly came into view at the opposite end of the long hallway.

"Officer Caldwell," she called out to him.

"Hey, Colette." In five long strides, he was before her with a concerned look. "Is everything all right? Do you need something?"

"I need to find Etienne as quickly as possible," she replied urgently.

"I think he's in his office. Come on, I'll take you there."

She fell into step next to the tall, lean, youthful officer, her excitement burning inside her. They didn't go far before he stopped at a closed door and knocked.

Etienne's voice drifted from inside, bidding them enter.

J.T. stepped aside and gestured for her to go in.

"Thanks," she told him and opened the door.

Etienne sat behind a large desk, but at the sight of her, he rose in surprise. "Colette, is everything okay?"

"It was a basement, Etienne," she said with excitement. "We were all being held in a basement with concrete walls."

"Are you sure?" His eyes lit up.

"I'm positive. We weren't being held in the swamp at all. It was definitely a regular basement. The memory just came to me. This will help, won't it?"

"Oh, honey, this definitely helps," he replied. "All of our searches have been in the swamp. But it sounds like we need to change all that now." He walked around his desk and pulled her into his arms. "This is great, Colette," he murmured into her ear.

She thought he was about to release her when his lips claimed hers in an unexpected kiss. She leaned closer to him, reveling in the fire his mouth created against hers.

The kiss lasted only a moment, and then he stepped back from her. "You've just given us a whole new direction to take the investigation. Now, honey, you go back to your room, and I'll get to work."

"I hope you find it. I hope you find the right basement, Etienne," she said fervently and then turned and left his office.

As she walked back down the hall to the interview

room, her lips still burned with the imprint of his. As much as she had enjoyed the kiss, it also made her sad.

It broke her heart a little bit, knowing that he hadn't kissed her because he loved her. He had kissed her because she had brought him a memory. It merely confirmed that the memories were what he was after... and nothing more.

ETIENNE IMMEDIATELY CALLED TREY, Michael and Joel into his office. He didn't want to think about his motive for kissing Colette. It had been completely spontaneous. Merely due to his excitement and the fact that she had just looked so damn kissable.

Right now, his focus was on the information she'd brought him. Basements were not all that common in Crystal Cove. The water level excluded most houses from having them, but there were some homes on higher ground that did.

"All this time we were sure the victims were being held someplace in the swamp," Joel said.

"They disappeared in the swamp. It was a good bet that they were being held there too," Trey said.

"Apparently, we were all wrong," Etienne replied. "Michael, I'd like you to go check with the city's assessment office and get the addresses for all the homes and businesses that have basements in town. Once we have those addresses, we'll contact Judge Cooke about search warrants for each place."

He felt a new energy roar inside his veins, an energy that snapped in the air. He saw the fire of renewed vigor in the eyes and posture of his officers. They all were hungry for a win. Hopefully this would be the ultimate win. Perhaps by the end of the day they'd have the perpetrator behind bars and the victims all saved.

Michael left to get the addresses. While they waited for his return, Etienne pulled out a large map of the city and placed it on his desk. Together he, Trey and Joel studied the map.

"It's obvious the places under sea level will not have basements," Etienne said.

"So, that pretty much takes out this whole area," Trey said, running his finger over a particular neighborhood.

"But on this side of town, the houses are high enough on land to potentially have basements," Joel said and indicated another area on the map.

"Thank God we got this new tip or memory or whatever from Colette," Trey said.

"Otherwise, we'd still be spinning our wheels out in the swamp," Etienne replied.

It took almost forty-five minutes for Michael to return. The search had yielded six addresses of homes that had basements. Etienne immediately contacted Judge Cooke to get the search warrants he needed. Thankfully, the judge was a friend to the prosecution, and after learning about Colette's new memory, he immediately granted the search warrants.

"Here's what we're going to do. We'll go together to each address. I want each of you to be prepared for anything. As we go into each basement, we don't know what we might be facing," Etienne said. "Keep in mind that it's possible our missing people will be there. We have to go in with great care so none of them get hurt in the process. Trey, you ride with me. Michael and Joel, you follow."

Etienne quickly popped into the interview room to tell Colette he was leaving. He also spoke to J.T. and Annie and told them to keep an eye on her.

Electricity jolted through his veins as he and Trey got into his vehicle.

"This takes our two potential suspects off our list," Trey said once they were on their way to the first house.

"I seriously doubt that Levi Morel or Pierre Gusman would have access to a basement here in town," Etienne replied. He hit the center of his steering wheel. "Damn, I can't believe how wrong we've been about this case from the very beginning and how much time we've wasted searching in the swamp."

"We followed logic," Trey said in protest. "Etienne, it was only logical that a person from the swamp was kidnapping those people and hiding them someplace. And it was only logical that he'd be hiding them in the swamp, where he was most comfortable."

"So, what he must be doing is knocking his victims out in the swamp and then loading them into a vehicle to bring them to a basement in town. Too bad we don't have security cameras in the parking area outside the swamp."

"Yeah, that would have been helpful."

They were headed to 825 N.E. Cypress Drive…the home of Tommy Radcliffe. Thankfully, it was Sunday, so most of the homeowners should be in their houses. "And just because Tommy is the prosecuting attorney doesn't mean he gets an automatic pass."

"Who knows what's in the mind of the perp? He could be a well-respected man around town during the day, yet at night he could have demons that for some reason or another have him doing these crimes," Trey replied.

"I'd still love to know the motive for these disappearances," Etienne replied. "Why is he taking these people and holding them? For what purpose? What's his end game?"

"Who knows? Maybe his dog or cat or his pet canary is talking to him and telling him to kidnap all these people," Trey said wryly.

Etienne released a small laugh. "I don't think our perp is that insane. Once we catch him, let's hope he doesn't use his talking canary as a defense."

"I would think it'd be difficult for him to use an insanity defense. He obviously knows right from wrong and has gone to great lengths to hide these crimes from law enforcement," Trey replied.

They fell quiet as Etienne pulled into Tommy Radcliffe's driveway. The house was an old but well-kept two-story painted a light gray with black trim.

The other patrol car pulled in behind Etienne, and all four men got out of their vehicles.

"Remember, be ready for anything," Etienne told the others, and he led them up the stairs to the front door.

He knocked and waited for a response. After a few moments passed, he knocked again, this time a little harder.

The door flew open, and Tommy looked at all of them in surprise. "Chief…what's going on here?" he asked with obvious confusion. Despite it being Sunday, the slightly portly man was clad in black dress slacks and a crisp white shirt.

"Tommy, we have a search warrant to check out your basement," Etienne said and pulled the warrant out of his pocket.

"My basement? Why? Wait...you think I have something to do with the kidnappings?" Tommy said with a touch of outrage. "Are you out of your mind? I'm the prosecuting attorney in this town. I'm a respectable man, not a criminal."

"It's nothing personal, Tommy. We have information that the kidnapped are being held in a basement, so we're checking all the basements in town, no matter who they belong to," Etienne explained.

Tommy took the warrant from Etienne and then opened his door wide enough to let them all in. "The door to the basement is in the kitchen. Knock yourselves out." He walked over to the sofa and sat, now appearing calm and unbothered.

Etienne and his men went through the living room and into the kitchen where a door obviously led to the basement. Etienne opened it and listened. Hearing nothing, he started down the stairs, followed closely by Trey and the other men.

Etienne hadn't expected to find anything here, and he didn't. The basement walls were covered with wood paneling, and a sofa and chair faced a television.

From Tommy's house they headed to Dr. Dwight Maison's home, another place where Etienne expected nothing and found nothing. By that time, it was noon, and he called the office to make sure somebody got Colette lunch.

The men grabbed burgers at Big D's, then headed to 9509 N.E. Tupelo Lane. The owner of the home was Jason Maynard, known around town as a computer guru. Etienne didn't know the man well, but Jason had a reputation of being extremely bright and a loner.

Once again, adrenaline raced through Etienne as he knocked on the door.

Jason answered almost immediately. "Just don't touch anything down there," he said as he led them to the basement door.

Downstairs there were tables with computers in various stages of disrepair. "I fix them for people," Jason explained. "That's my business...repairing computers and cell phones, among other things."

They were halfway through the list of addresses, but hopefully the one they sought was still within reach. Next up was the home of Wesley Simone, now occupied by his widow, Millie.

Wesley had been a successful businessman who, unfortunately, had begun to dabble in illegal drugs. He was murdered by a dope dealer he owed money to. Initially, Heather LaCrae, the woman found covered in blood next to Wesley's dead body, had been charged with the crime. Her defense attorney, Nick Monroe, had worked hard to prove her innocence. In the end, she was exonerated of all the charges against her. While working on the case, Heather and Nick had fallen in love, and now were a happy couple planning a wedding.

Love had certainly been in the air in Crystal Cove

for the past couple months. First Angel Marchant had found her forever person, and then Heather had found hers. Cupid had been around the small town, but he'd certainly not been around Etienne, nor did Etienne want him around.

The Simone home was another large, old two-story, and Millie answered the door on the second knock. Since her husband's murder, Millie had lost weight and wore a sadness that was heartbreaking. She had professed to know nothing about her husband's drug deals and had been as stunned as everyone else when the truth about Wesley had come out.

There was no way Etienne believed Millie would have anything to do with the disappearances from the swamp, but Wesley and Millie had three big, strapping sons who would have access to the basement.

However, again it was a bust. The basement held nothing but old furniture covered with sheets and random boxes.

Two more addresses. Etienne tightened his hands on the steering wheel as they drove to the next to last house on the list.

"It has to be one of these last two," Trey said.

"Let's hope so," Etienne replied. The excitement he had started with had diminished a bit with each basement cleared. "If this doesn't pan out, then I really don't know where we go from here."

"Maybe Colette will remember more," Trey said.

"Her memories are starting to come back, but they are returning very slowly," Etienne replied.

"She remembered a basement, so we're going to find it in the next hour or so," Trey said optimistically.

It was just after four now. There was no way he'd be back at the station by five. Once again, he called one of his officers and arranged for Colette to order some dinner from the café. By the time he finished up the day, it would be too late for her to cook dinner at home.

Minutes later, they pulled up into the driveway of Lincoln Mayfield's home. Lincoln was father to the hotheaded, loudmouthed Brett, who lived here with his father and mother.

The home was one of the largest in Crystal Creek, a two-story painted forest green with white trim. Etienne knocked on the door, and after a moment it was opened by Lincoln. He was a tall, good-looking older man with graying hair and piercing blue eyes.

"This is utterly preposterous," he said when Etienne explained why they were there. "Why on earth do I have to let you into my home?"

"Lincoln, I have a search warrant," Etienne said.

"And why do I have to honor your search warrant?" He pinned Etienne with an arrogant glare.

"If you don't allow us to conduct this search, then I'll have to arrest you," Etienne replied as he held the man's gaze. Why would Lincoln kick up such a fuss?

He held Etienne's gaze for another minute, then opened the door wider. "I'll tell you right now, I don't know the condition of the basement. I don't know what goes on down there. That's Brett's space, and I don't ever go down there."

"Where is Brett now?" Etienne asked.

"He's someplace north of town working on a project," Lincoln replied.

The only information the basement yielded was the fact that Brett lived like a pig. Dirty clothes were strewn around the room along with old fast-food wrappers and rusty construction tools.

Etienne's stomach tightened as they drove to the last location. *This has to be it*, he thought. This absolutely has to be the place. The house was owned by Arnold Swan, a single businessman that Etienne didn't know other than seeing him around town.

It's got to be here, he thought again as he knocked on the door. It was now after five o'clock, and it felt as if the day had gone on forever.

As he waited for his knock to be answered, despite the long hours of the day, he once again felt energized and ready to make an arrest. He exchanged a look with Trey, who appeared just as ready. All his men seemed on high alert, believing this last basement was the one holding their victims… This was the basement where Colette had been held and beaten.

Arnold opened the door. He was a tall man with broad shoulders.

"Mr. Swan…we have a search warrant for your basement," Etienne said.

"For what? What are you specifically searching for?" Arnold's eyes suddenly widened and then narrowed. "Oh wait, I guess this means I'm the Swamp Soul Stealer." He laughed. It was a nasty sound that instantly raised Etienne's hackles.

"We're just interested in looking in your basement," Etienne replied evenly.

"I hear there's a recall effort going on against you. Some people around here want to kick your butt right out of office," Arnold said.

"I hear the same thing, but it hasn't happened yet. I'm still the chief of police, and I'm still working this case. Now, if you would just guide us to your basement, I would appreciate it," Etienne replied evenly. Arnold was definitely a piece of work, but Etienne kept his temper in check.

After going back and forth for several more minutes, Arnold finally opened his door and led them to the kitchen where there was a door.

"I hope I got all those victims hid real good in the basement," Arnold said sarcastically.

"Mr. Swan, this is nothing to joke about," Trey said. Etienne heard the barely suppressed anger in his friend's voice.

The minute he opened the basement door, Etienne knew there was nothing there. His heart sank as he saw the sofa and love seat, along with a television mounted on the wall. It was an ordinary rec room, not a lair holding abused, kidnapped people.

"I wanted to punch that guy in his face," Trey said as they drove back to the station.

"Yeah, he's definitely an unpleasant man," Etienne replied. "It's no wonder he isn't married. He's somebody only a mother could love."

Etienne was positively sick with defeat. All the energy that had driven him all day long was gone now, crushed by the failure of the searches. He'd been so sure the perp would be behind bars by now. Instead, they were out of basements and back to square one, and he had never felt so ill.

It was almost 6:30 p.m. when he got back to the office.

Colette already had her computer packed up, and she greeted him with a tentative smile.

He shook his head, and her smile fell away. "Let's get out of here," he said dispiritedly.

She immediately got up and followed him down the hall. Once outside, he held her close against his side until she was safely in the car. He didn't feel like talking on the way home, and thankfully she seemed to read his mood and was silent herself. They got back home and went into the living room where he sank down on the sofa.

"Have you eaten?" she asked, breaking the silence at last.

"No, but I'm not hungry," he replied. "What about you? Did you eat?"

"I did." She walked over and stopped before him. She reached for his hand and pulled him up to stand in front of her. Then she leaned into him and wrapped her arms around his neck. She stared into his eyes for a long moment, then nestled her head into the hollow of his throat.

He wanted to push her away. He knew he needed to push her away, but there was sweet comfort in her arms...in the warmth and softness of her body. So, even knowing it was wrong, he pulled her closer to him and allowed her to be a soft place for him to fall.

Chapter Eleven

Colette knew Etienne was devastated by the day's lack of results. She hoped holding him in her arms would take away some of the sting of defeat.

He held her tight against him and she responded in kind. All she wanted to do was comfort him and take away the deep shadows of failure that darkened his gaze. They held each other for several long minutes and then he raised his head and looked deep in her eyes. Then he kissed her.

The kiss was filled with a wild hunger and more than the hint of a desperate need.

In this moment she wanted to give him whatever he needed, so when he grabbed her hand and led her down the hallway and into his bedroom, she went willingly...eagerly.

He kissed her once again, and then they were undressing in a frenzy. Clothes flew off, and he yanked down the bedspread, gray eyes smoldering, and stretched her across the bed.

There was little foreplay before he took her, but she didn't need any. Instead, there was a ravenous hunger and a fierce need that radiated from him. He pumped into her quickly, and she grabbed his buttocks to encourage him. Fast and frantic, he moved in and out of her.

She was suddenly overcome with a fierce climax that left her weak and gasping his name. He found his own release soon after, groaning and then collapsing breathlessly next to her on the bed.

After several long minutes, he released a deep sigh. "I'm so sorry, Colette. I... I just used you," he said.

"I know. It's okay," she replied softly.

He rolled over on his side and propped himself up on one elbow. He reached out and gently shoved a strand of her hair away from her eyes.

"Why did you allow me to do that?" he asked, his eyes dark and enigmatic. "Why would you let any man use you that way?"

"Etienne, you aren't any man, and I wanted you to use me. Trust me, if I had felt differently, then we wouldn't be here right now. I care about you, and I knew you were in a really bad place. You don't have to apologize to me, Etienne. I wanted to be with you, I wanted to comfort you in any way I could."

He held her gaze for another long moment and then rolled away from her and sat up. "Why don't we get dressed and go back to the living room?" He picked up his clothing from the floor and disappeared into an en suite bathroom.

She got her clothing and padded down the hallway to the bathroom she always used. Once she was dressed, she went out to the living room where he was already seated in his recliner.

She settled on the sofa and looked at him. "I don't believe my memory was a false one. I still think we were being held in a basement."

"I don't believe your memory was false either. However, we checked out six basements today, all that were listed in the assessor's office," he replied. He looked completely exhausted, lines of stress etching across his forehead and other lines deepening at the outer corners of his eyes. "And we found nothing...absolutely nothing."

"Is it possible the assessor is behind in their record-keeping? That maybe some new construction hasn't been listed there yet?" she asked.

He released a deep sigh and ran a hand through his hair. "At this point, I guess anything is possible. We'll see what we can figure out in the morning. Somehow, somewhere, we're missing something."

"Maybe I'll remember something more that will be more help in pinpointing the location," she replied, angry with herself that her memories were coming to her so slowly.

He cast her a tired smile. "I know you're doing the best you can, Colette."

"But it's not good enough," she replied in disgust and then stood. "Now, how about I make you a sandwich? You don't even have to get out of your chair. I'll bring it in here for you to eat, and, Etienne, you do need to eat something."

"I guess I could eat a sandwich," he replied, weariness evident in his voice.

"I'll be right back." She went into the kitchen where

she made him a thick ham-and-cheese sandwich, added a handful of potato chips to the plate and grabbed a soda from the refrigerator. She went back into the living room and handed him the plate and soda.

"Thanks," he said. "What did you have for dinner?"

"The meat loaf special from the café," she replied.

"How was it?" He took a bite of the sandwich.

"It was good. It came with mashed potatoes, corn and applesauce," she replied. "You should be eating something like that instead of a sandwich."

"This sandwich is fine for tonight." For the next few minutes, they both were silent as he ate. The only sound in the room was him crunching on potato chips.

She still felt defeat radiating from him. It had to have been so frustrating to get to the last basement on their list and realize there was nothing there.

There had to still be a basement somewhere out there that was a den of evil with victims who had been beaten and starved. That basement must have somehow slipped through the cracks today. Tomorrow was another day. Hopefully Etienne and his men would find it.

"Thanks," Etienne said again when he'd finished eating. "I thought I wasn't hungry, but that tasted really good."

"Do you want another one?"

"No, thanks. I'm good." He set the plate on the end table next to him and stared off to the space over her left shoulder.

"Etienne, you're going to get him," she said softly.

He focused his gaze back on her. "I hope so. I need to find him soon because I worry about the victims who are being held." He frowned. "If he's beating them as badly as you were beaten, then one day longer in captivity is too damn long."

"He seemed to take a special pleasure in beating me," she replied thoughtfully.

"Is that a memory of yours?" he asked curiously.

"Maybe a bit of one. I just remember wondering why he seemed hell-bent on beating me more than the others... Not that I wished it on the others."

"I'm just so damn sorry you had to go through it." His gaze lingered on her. "You were so broken when you were found. We weren't sure you were even going to make it."

"It's amazing how the will to survive can keep a person alive," she replied.

"Have you written about your experiences with all this?" he asked curiously.

"No, not yet. I won't write about it until the Swamp Soul Stealer is in jail and all the vanished have been found again," she replied. "Now, even though it's relatively early, why don't we get ready for bed? And if you want me to, I'll give you a nice, relaxing back rub to send you off to sleep."

He looked at her in surprise. "Now, that's an offer too good to refuse." He got out of his chair and headed to his bedroom.

She took his plate back into the kitchen and placed it in the dishwasher, then went to her room and changed into a soft light pink nightshirt.

He was already in his bed and was facedown with his bare back exposed. She got onto the bed next to him and began running a hand down his warm, beautiful skin. Up and down, she caressed his back and slowly felt the tight knots of tension melt away beneath her ministrations. She loved just touching his skin. Despite the long day, she still smelled a whisper of his cologne.

After several minutes, he rolled over and looked at her. "Thank you, that felt amazing." He gazed at her for several long moments. "Stay in here with me for the night?"

As an answer, she simply slid beneath the sheets next to him. He reached out and turned off the lamp on the nightstand. Immediately, he pulled her against him as he spooned around her back.

She snuggled in against him, and he tightened his arm around her waist. "Colette," he whispered. "When you find your special person, you're going to make him a terrific wife."

"Thanks," she replied and fought against a sudden burn of tears. She'd already found her special person. She was in his arms right this very minute.

But apparently, she wasn't his special person. When this case was solved, it was going to take her a very long time to get over the heartbreak of loving Etienne Savoie.

HE WAS PARKED just down the street from the lawman's home. He'd been watching them each evening when they returned from the police station. He wasn't fool enough to try to get at her while she was there, surrounded by cops.

He had decided he no longer wanted to kill her. What

he really wanted was for her to be back in her little cell where he could beat her whenever he wanted.

The bitch reminded him so much of the swamp whore who had been his father's lover for years. While Colette had been in his captivity, he'd beaten her like he'd wanted to beat the woman who destroyed his family and broke his mother.

He wanted that again. He wanted her back so he could beat her all over again. That would be so much better than killing her and ending it with her. Even now, just thinking about having her back in captivity shot a wild wave of sweet anticipation through him.

Yes, he'd been watching and learning their habits and he now thought he knew a way to get to her. But he wanted to think about it some more and make sure it was possible.

One night very soon, he'd make his move. Hopefully when it was all over, Colette would again be in his basement and he would be in control of her.

Once again, a sweet rush of pleasure roared through him as he thought of beating the beauty right out of her.

ETIENNE SAT AT his desk with Trey and Joel by his side as they studied the map of the city. Earlier in the day, Joel had gone back to the assessor's office where the clerk admitted that the records hadn't been updated for several years.

What Etienne and his men were looking at now were areas in the city and the surrounding outskirts that would have the appropriate land height to have a basement.

"This area here might have basements," Joel said and pointed to an area on the north side of town. "I know there's a couple of relatively new homes there."

"Let's get addresses for those," Etienne said.

"And here's another area that we might need to put on our search list," Trey said and pointed to the map. "There are a few new homes there as well."

"Again, let's put together a list of addresses as soon as possible so we can get them to Judge Cooke for more search warrants," Etienne said.

Minutes later Joel left to look at city records and get the addresses of places they needed to search.

"You doing okay?" Trey asked Etienne with concern when it was just the two of them in the office.

"Yeah, I'm doing all right," Etienne replied. "I'll admit last night I wasn't doing so great, but I'm feeling much better today." His phone beeped, and he looked at the text, then looked up at Trey. "The mayor is on his way in to talk to me."

"Then I'll get out of here," Trey replied. "Don't let him get to you."

Etienne released a dry laugh. "I doubt he's coming in to tell me how great I am."

"Just keep your head up," Trey said and then he left the office.

A few moments later, after a sharp knock on the door, Allen Larrick walked in.

Etienne immediately rose and held out his hand. "Mayor Larrick," he said in greeting, and the two men shook hands.

Allen was a short, squat man who was very popular

in the small town. He was a glad-handing, baby-kissing kind of man who had always been very supportive of Etienne and the police department.

He now sat across from Etienne and wore a small frown on his plump face. "Etienne, I've pretty much stayed out of your business on this whole Swamp Soul Stealer case."

"And I've appreciated that," Etienne replied.

"I know you and your officers are doing everything possible to catch this creep. How is the investigation going?"

"Hopefully we're getting closer to catching him. Colette remembered that she had been held in a basement, so we spent all day yesterday checking out basements around town. Unfortunately, those searches didn't yield the results we wanted. Today we're planning on checking out more basements in hopes of finding this madman's lair."

"That sounds quite promising," Allen replied.

"We're getting closer, Allen. I feel like we're definitely getting closer to finding this creep," Etienne said firmly.

"Now that's what I like to hear," Allen replied with one of his trademark wide smiles. "I just felt like it was my duty to come and check in with you."

"Thank you for not putting additional pressure on me. Trust me, I feel the heavy pressure of people wanting this man caught and the victims all to be saved."

"You're a good man, Etienne. I have all the faith in the world in you."

"Thanks. Nobody wants this guy in jail more than

me. If there was any way to catch him before now, I would have done so. However, this has been a tough one with no clues to follow and no leads to guide us in the investigation."

"I think everyone in town knows this has been a tough one," Allen replied sympathetically.

"But I also know there are some people who are unhappy with me. I've heard about the recall effort."

Allen waved his pudgy hand. "Don't worry about it, Etienne. It's all just a bunch of nonsense by a disgruntled few." He rose, and Etienne did as well. "The people of Crystal Cove are still firmly behind you, and we're good, Etienne. I just thought it was time I did a little check-in."

"I appreciate it," Etienne replied. The two men shook hands again, and Allen left the office.

Etienne leaned back in his chair and breathed a sigh of relief. His conversation with the mayor could have been much more difficult. Thank God, Allen continued to be a support rather than a hindrance.

With the office quiet for the moment, Etienne's thoughts went to Colette. She seemed to have known exactly what he'd needed the night before. He felt terrible for the way he had taken her...so hard and fast. But he'd needed the mindlessness of sex to alleviate the tremendous pressure of failure inside him.

He didn't want to think about how nice it had been to sleep with her in his arms. Her body had been so warm, and her scent had swirled around in his head. For the first time in a very long time, he had slept... really slept in his bed.

He knew the reason for his good sleep was her. She had tended to every need he'd had last night. The sandwich had fed his belly, and the sex and the back rub had fed his very soul.

Damn, his feelings toward her were a tangled mess. He knew she believed herself in love with him, but her feelings toward him were probably a tangled mess too. They'd been in close proximity for too long. She saw him as her protector, and he wanted her memories to return.

Once this was all over, their connection would probably end. She would no longer need him to protect her, and he would no longer need her memories.

He would miss her.

The thought surprised him, but it was true. He would miss their conversations in the evenings. He would definitely miss her full-bodied laughter. She had filled his house with a liveliness and an energy it had been missing since he'd bought the place.

A knock on his door sounded, and he called out a welcome. Trey came back in, a hesitant expression on his features. "How did it go with Larrick?"

"Good," Etienne replied.

"Ah, that's great," Trey said as his expression cleared. "I was afraid he was here to chew you out."

"No matter how much anyone chews me out, that won't get us any results," Etienne replied. "But he really just stopped in to check the progress of the investigation."

"Did you tell him about the basement tip?"

"I did," Etienne replied. "I told him I thought we

were getting very close to finding this creep and freeing the captives. Let's hope that's true and the victims are all still alive."

"And let's hope Joel comes back with the addresses of the places we need to check out," Trey replied.

"Yeah, and we get through them all quickly," Etienne said.

"And with success by the end of the day," Trey said optimistically.

Joel returned almost an hour later with the addresses of ten homes. They didn't know if these places had basements or not, but they would know within hours.

The addresses were faxed to Judge Cooke with the request for search warrants for each of them. Thankfully, the judge responded quickly. Once they received the warrants, it was Etienne, Joel, Trey and Michael who took off in two patrol cars to check the first address on the list.

The day was another bust, and at five o'clock Etienne collected Colette to go home.

"No luck?" she asked once they were in the car.

"None. We only found two more basements, and needless to say, neither of them was the place we wanted," he replied. The defeat today was less heavy than the day before. Maybe because at this point, he'd come to expect defeat.

"It looks like it's going to storm," she said.

The evening had turned preternaturally dark with black, angry clouds filling the sky and swallowing up any hint of the sun. "Yeah, the forecast was for some rain and thunderstorms this evening," he replied.

"It's spooky for it to be so dark at this time of day," she replied.

"Spooky? Are you scared of storms?" he asked with a glance at her. She looked so pretty in jeans and a hot pink blouse with her hair loose down her back.

"Maybe just a little bit even though I know it's silly," she replied. "Are you hungry?" she asked in an obvious effort to change the topic of conversation.

"I could eat," he replied. "What's on the menu?"

"Chicken cutlets with scalloped potatoes and corn."

"Sounds good to me," he replied. It was important to him that tonight they stay on an even keel with no deep emotions making unwise decisions for him.

"They were jail-like cells…where he kept us," she said suddenly. "The basement was full of these wooden little cells with some of us chained to the wall and others free inside their tiny cages."

He glanced at her in surprise. "Another memory?"

She looked surprised herself. "Just a little snippet. It popped into my head just now. But why don't I see his face in the memories that are returning?"

"I don't know. Maybe the vision of him would still be too traumatic for you, so your brain is still protecting you," he replied.

"Well, I wish it would stop it." She sighed heavily. "I just wish my memories would come back all at once."

"Every little bit you get is helpful," he replied encouragingly. "Don't beat up on yourself, Colette."

"I just want to help so badly."

"And you are. Without your memory, we'd still be spinning our wheels out in the swamp." He turned up his street, his headlights illuminating the road. When he turned into his driveway, he punched the button on his visor to raise the garage door.

"It's nice to be home before the rain," she said.

"There is that," he agreed. He pulled into the garage and pushed the button again to close the garage door. As the two of them got out of the car, there was a sudden flash of movement, and the garage door opened up once again.

For a brief moment Etienne's brain couldn't process what was going on, then reality slammed into him.

Dammit, the creep had gotten in. Etienne fumbled for his gun as he yelled at Colette to get inside the house and lock the door. Before he could do anything else, a shot rang out. A piercing pain stabbed through his upper arm and momentarily stole his breath away.

At the same time the man—dressed all in black and with a ski mask hiding his features—grabbed hold of Colette's arm and yanked her out of the garage. She screamed, and the sound of her terror ripped through Etienne's very soul.

Still gasping with pain, he ran after them, but by the time he got out of the garage he didn't see them anywhere. Nor did he hear any more of Colette's cries for help. It was as if the dark night had swallowed them up whole.

Etienne got on his phone and called in all his officers, then he found a clean cloth in his tool chest and wrapped it firmly around the injury in his upper arm.

The wound was painful and bleeding quite a bit. He knew he probably needed to go to the hospital to get it tended to, but that was the last place he was going while Colette was missing.

Damn, it had all happened so fast. He'd been so taken by surprise and so ill-prepared for the attack. He couldn't believe she was again in the custody of the Swamp Soul Stealer. Oh God, was she already dead? Had the man already killed her, and that was why her cries had stopped so abruptly?

Etienne was supposed to have protected her, and he'd failed. Dammit, he had failed. His heart crashed against his ribs in a frantic rhythm. He stood outside to wait for his men to arrive and fought back the thick emotion that attempted to crawl up the back of his throat.

Would they be able to find her? Or was it already too late, and they would simply find her body?

HE'D DONE IT. He yanked the ski mask off his head and tossed it on top of the drugged woman slumped in the passenger seat next to him.

The thrill of success rushed through him. The whole thing had gone exactly as he planned. The minute the garage door went up, he'd rushed inside and placed a small box in front of the sensor so that the door wouldn't close. And now she was his once again.

He glanced over at her and tightened his hands around the steering wheel. She looked so much like Sonya, the woman who'd had the yearslong affair with his father.

The affair had only ended when Sonya was killed in a car accident. But by that time the damage had already been done. Years of love and devotion that should have belonged to his mother had been stolen away by the swamp whore who had infatuated his father.

How many nights had he heard his mother weeping alone in her room while his father was out gallivanting with his swamp bitch? How many days had his mother been unable to get out of bed because of the utter grief that consumed her?

He didn't know why she had stayed with his father. She should have left him when the affair first began. But she hadn't. Love and devotion had kept her with him even though he didn't deserve it, didn't deserve her.

He wanted to punch Colette in her beautiful face. "Self-control," he said aloud. He needed to display some self-control right now. It wasn't the right time for beating her. She was drugged and out of it. He wanted her fully conscious when he hit her. But the drug would only keep her unconscious for a short period of time, and then he would not only beat her, but he needed to figure out a way to punish her for escaping him in the first place.

Thank God she hadn't remembered anything that would lead to him. Otherwise, he would already be under arrest. Thank God he'd gotten to her before all of her memories had returned.

What he needed to do right now was get back to the basement as quickly as possible. It wouldn't take long before cops would be roaming the streets and checking vehicles. He needed to get home before he got caught up in the manhunt he knew was about to happen.

He laughed out loud. He was so freaking proud of

himself. He had managed to kidnap a woman right under the nose of the chief of police.

He wished he had a friend he could crow to, somebody who would see his absolute genius and appreciate it. While he had lots of good friends, he knew better than to talk about this part of his life with anyone.

All he wanted to do now was get Colette back in her little cage where he could take her out and play with her at will.

"Let the games begin," he said and then laughed with the sweet anticipation of what was to come.

Chapter Twelve

"You need to go to the hospital," Trey said to Etienne. The two men stood in front of Etienne's house while other officers combed the area looking for anything that might help them find Colette. Others were driving the streets in search of the perp and his captive.

"I'll go to the hospital once Colette is found safe and sound," Etienne replied firmly.

"That's got to be painful as hell," Trey said, gesturing to Etienne's gunshot wound.

At that moment a steak of lightning lit the sky, followed by a clap of thunder.

"It's not too bad," Etienne replied. "It's just a graze." The pain in his upper arm didn't even begin to compete with the utter pain in his heart. Colette was gone, in the grasp of the monster who had nearly beaten her to death the last time he had her. To make matters worse, a storm was upon them. Colette was afraid of storms. Somehow that made everything worse.

"Let's head into the office," Etienne said. "It will make it easier for me to keep track of the search." He took hold of Trey's arm. "We've got to find her, man," he said fervently. "She's in serious danger."

"We'll find her, Etienne," Trey replied just as fervently. "I swear we're going to find her."

Etienne dropped his hand from Trey's arm and released a deep, shaky sigh. "Okay, let's get to the office."

A few minutes later Etienne was in his car and headed toward the police station. As he drove, he looked hard at any car on the street.

The Swamp Soul Stealer had to have drugged her and then carried her to a waiting vehicle. That would explain her sudden silence and their immediate disappearance.

Why hadn't Etienne realized that moment of vulnerability when the garage door was closing? Why hadn't he seen that as a potential danger? It hadn't even entered his mind that the moment the garage door went up, somebody could get in. But he hadn't seen it, and now he was paying the consequences.

No, she was paying the consequences. That thought shattered his heart into a million pieces.

He reached the police station, and he and Trey went straight to his office where he pulled out the city map. From here, he should be able to coordinate a full citywide search. He wanted his officers checking out cars and knocking on doors. He wanted this little town to be torn apart in the search for Colette.

While he'd been waiting for his men to arrive at his house, he'd interviewed all his neighbors to see if they had witnessed anything. Unfortunately, none of them had.

Another boom of thunder shook the building. Where was she now? Was she back in her cage in a basement, or would they find her dead body tossed on the side of the road someplace? Etienne squeezed his eyes tightly closed as another rush of emotion threatened to consume him.

He needed to keep his emotions in check right now. Colette didn't need a weepy, emotional man searching for her. She'd want him to be strong and focused.

As his officers checked in with him, he formed a grid search with some of the men starting at the south end of town and others at the north end. They were instructed to knock on every door and check every building. He had other officers checking cars for the missing woman.

The minutes ticked by, and as time passed, Etienne's hope for finding her began to wane. One by one his men checked in with nothing to report.

Searing pain still burned in his arm, but it was nothing compared to the agony that roared through his heart. By midnight, the storm had passed overhead, and Etienne came to the painful conclusion that the searches had yielded nothing.

He sat at his desk with Trey in the chair facing him. "She said they were all held in a basement," he said, trying to think through his heartbreak.

"But we've checked all the basements," Trey replied.

"Somehow, someway, we've missed one," Etienne said in abject frustration.

"I agree, but damned if I know where it is," Trey replied. "What else did she tell you? Did she have more memories about the place where she was held?"

Etienne frowned thoughtfully. "She said the basement had little cells in it where the people were held. However, she was often chained to the wall in her little cell." The idea of her being back in that place of nightmares positively killed him.

"Cells? Like little jail cells?" Trey asked.

Etienne nodded. "Only she said the cells were constructed of wood."

"Wood?" Trey frowned. "So the guy has to know his way around building things."

Etienne's mind whirled. The Swamp Soul Stealer had to be a big man to carry the victims from the swamp to his vehicle. He was handy at building things.

A name suddenly popped into his brain.

"Brett Mayfield," he said and stared at Trey. Was it possible the loudmouthed handyman was behind all this?

Trey's frown deepened. "But he lives with his mother and father, and we checked the basement there."

Etienne got up from his chair, a burst of adrenaline exploding inside him. "I think we need to have a long chat with Brett."

By the time Etienne got a couple more officers with him, it was almost one o'clock in the morning. But time had no meaning to him as long as Colette was gone.

Trey rode with him, and Joel and Michael followed in their own car. Etienne was grateful that all his officers were still working, no matter how many hours they had already put into the day. They had all come out to help find Colette.

As he headed to Lincoln Mayfield's home, Etienne's heart beat a million miles a minute. Was it possible this was it? Was it possible Brett was the Swamp Soul Stealer? Etienne had no idea where Brett would be keeping the captives. He reminded himself it was equally possible Brett wasn't the kidnapper.

But one thing was certain, if he'd hurt Colette, Etienne would have no problem putting a bullet in the center of the man's evil soul. And hopefully when they found Colette, they would find all the others being held captive.

He clenched the steering wheel tightly as he drove through the night. When they reached the large house, the four of them got out of their cars and approached the front door.

Etienne knocked. They waited for several moments, and then he knocked again more loudly. Finally, he heard movement inside, and the door flew open.

"Chief Savoie, do you have any idea what time it is?" Lincoln asked indignantly.

"I know it's late, and I apologize for that," Etienne replied.

"What's so damned important it couldn't wait until morning?" Lincoln asked. He pulled a blue-checkered robe closely around him.

"We need to talk to Brett," Etienne said.

Lincoln frowned. "What has the poor excuse for a son done now? Another bar fight? I swear that boy doesn't know how to keep his mouth shut. I told him I was done bailing him out of jail and paying his fines."

"We need to talk to him about another matter. Could you go get him for us?"

"He's not here."

Etienne frowned. "Do you know where he is?"

"If he's not in a bar somewhere, then he's probably out on his property," Lincoln replied.

"His property?" Etienne's heart beat a little bit faster. "And where is that?"

"On the north side of town, on Oak Drive. He's building a house for himself out there, and I can't wait to get him out of my basement."

Almost before the words were out of Lincoln's mouth, Etienne and Trey were running for the car. "New construction... That's how we missed it," Trey said eagerly.

"It's possible we're just on another wild-goose chase," Etienne said. "We don't even know if this house he's building has a basement."

"Admit it, this all feels right," Trey said, excitement filling his voice.

"It does feel right, but I'm almost afraid to get my hopes up. We've been disappointed in the past," Etienne replied. He was so afraid to hope. And he was so afraid that they might be too late for her.

He glanced in the rearview mirror, assured by the presence of Michael and Joel behind him. He was grateful for the extra man power. He had no idea what they might be walking into. If Brett was their man, then he could be quite dangerous. The last thing Etienne wanted was any kind of a hostage situation with the kidnapped victims.

He drove as fast as he could given the wet conditions of the streets. Lincoln hadn't given them an exact address, but Oak Drive was a short road with few homes on it. They should have no trouble finding a new house under construction.

Unfortunately, there wasn't a single ray of moonlight to aid them in the inky darkness of the night. When Etienne reached Oak Drive, he slowed to a snail's pace.

"You look on the right side of the street, and I'll look on the left," Etienne said.

"Bingo," Trey said when they hadn't gone far. Etienne braked and looked to the right.

The ranch-style house was framed in, and a bright light shone out the missing front door. None of the windows were in yet. There were only gaping holes where they would eventually be.

Etienne pulled to the curb and killed his headlights. In his rearview mirror, he saw Joel pull up right behind him and turn off his lights as well.

Etienne's chest tightened, and his mouth went completely dry. This had to be it. The monster's lair, where four men and four women including Colette were being held inside. At least he hoped Colette was here and not dead.

"We need to go in as quietly as possible, especially since we have no idea where Brett might be in the place," he said. "We need to get him in custody as quickly as we can…before he can use his captives as hostages."

"Agreed," Trey replied tersely.

"You and I will go in the front, and I'll have Joel and Michael circle around to the back."

The four men descended on the house. Etienne held his gun steadily before him. He would prefer not to have to kill the man, but if he was the Swamp Soul Stealer, then Etienne definitely wanted him in custody.

He entered through the empty front door into a room that would probably be the kitchen. He had just crossed the threshold when a door along another wall opened, and Brett appeared.

His eyes widened at the sight of Etienne. Then he turned and ran for a window, vaulting through the empty hole.

"Don't shoot!" Etienne cried out as he raced after him.

Thankfully, Joel and Michael held their fire, joining the chase for Brett. Etienne wanted him. This was a fantasy he'd dreamed about for the past five and a half months. This man had tormented his sleep and beleaguered his days.

"Halt!" he yelled at the man running ahead of him.

Despite the sharp pain in his upper arm, in spite of his desire to find Colette as quickly as possible, he raced after Brett, keeping the big man in view. He ignored the stitch in his side, the pain in his arm and simply ran, driven by the need to bring the man down.

Closer and closer, until he could hear Brett's loud gasps for air. Etienne holstered his gun, and when he was close enough, he jumped on Brett's back and took him down to the ground.

"Brett, it's over!" he yelled breathlessly, attempting to control the struggling man.

"Get the hell off me!" Brett exclaimed. "Why are you people on my property?"

Joel, Trey and Michael had reached them, and they pulled him to his feet.

"What the hell is going on here?" Brett asked as Trey handcuffed him.

"We're just here to check out your basement," Etienne replied.

"You have no right to do that. Do you have a search warrant?" Brett asked belligerently.

"Don't need one. You hear that, men? I just heard the cry of somebody in great distress," Etienne replied. "We need to check it out."

"You're a damn liar," Brett said, his brown eyes blazing with anger.

"Go on, Etienne. We've got him," Joel said.

"We'll put him in the back of our car," Michael added.

Etienne didn't have to be told twice. With his heart swelled up in his chest, he turned and ran back to the house, aware of Trey following close behind. He dashed into the kitchen and yanked open what had to be the basement door.

He knew immediately he had found the captives. Moans and groans came up the stairs. It was the sound of pain and human despair.

Etienne raced down the stairs and straight into a nightmare. "Get some ambulances out here," he called to Trey.

Just as Colette had described, there were small wooden cells where each captive was held.

A set of keys hung on the wall, and he grabbed them. He turned to the captives' cages, frantically seeking the one he most wanted to see. God, where was she? Was she even here? His heart banged unevenly in his chest.

"Etienne!" Her cry rose above the others and led him to the last cell.

Tears misted his eyes. Thank God...thank God, she was alive. He fumbled with the keys, trying desperately to find the one that would open the door. She was weeping, but thankfully she appeared to be in good shape.

He finally got the door open, and he pulled her out and into his arms. She clung to him, and despite the pain in his arm, he held her tightly against him.

It was finally over. The Swamp Soul Stealer was in custody at last, and the captives had been saved. Colette continued to weep, and Etienne tossed the keys to Trey.

"Open them all up, Trey. Let's get these people out of here," he said.

By this time, most of the other captives were crying with the relief at finally being saved.

"I've got ambulances coming, and I told J.T. to contact Black Bayou and have them send us some ambulances as well," Trey said.

"Good, we're going to need them." Etienne finally released Colette. The others needed him now.

As Trey unlocked the cells, Etienne checked the condition of each captive. Most of them were painfully thin, and the women appeared to be in worse shape than the men.

Finally, everyone was free from the cages that had held them. Etienne led the captives up the stairs and out of the house where they all got their first breath of fresh air.

"I thought we'd never get out of there," Luka Lurance exclaimed.

Sophia Fabre grabbed hold of Etienne's hand and cried. "Thank you…thank you," she said tearfully over and over again as she squeezed his hand tightly.

"I'm never going to take my mother for granted again," Kate Dirant said as tears coursed down her cheeks.

It didn't take too long for the first ambulance to arrive. The first person loaded in and taken away was Haley Chenevert, who appeared to have a broken arm among other bruises. After that, more ambulances arrived, and the captives were loaded up one at a time and taken to the hospital.

Colette went on one of the last ambulances. She didn't want to go, but Etienne insisted. He wanted her checked out by a doctor.

The vanished had finally been found, and they would get the medical help they needed. He prayed that they all would recover. The nightmare was truly over.

As the last ambulance pulled away, Etienne stood in the darkness of the night, and a deep relief washed over him. For the first time in months, he felt as if he could breathe.

"Now it's your turn to go to the hospital," Trey said firmly as he joined Etienne on Brett's front yard.

"We still need to process the crime scene," Etienne replied. Photos needed to be taken, and reports needed to be written.

"Etienne, we can take care of all that without you. You need to go and get that arm looked at," Trey replied firmly. "You've put if off for too long already."

The pain in his arm was still fairly intense. "Okay, I'll go now. Are you sure you guys have it here?"

"Positive, and we'll also process your garage as a crime scene... Now go."

Minutes later Etienne was in his car and headed to the hospital. His arm hadn't stopped hurting all day, and he'd had to change the bandage on it several times due to bleeding.

The last thing he wanted to do was take a doctor away from treating the people who had been pulled out of that hellhole of a basement. But he admitted he did need some medical help.

The emergency waiting room was filled with family members of the captives. They greeted him happily, joyously, and thanked him profusely for getting their loved ones back to safety.

Etienne was immediately taken to a small examining room where he sat and waited for a doctor to come in. As he waited, his head filled with thoughts of Colette.

She was free now. The danger had passed, and she was free to live her life without fear. Thankfully, she had remembered just enough to help them get Brett under arrest. Hopefully now she would never have to remember the rest of the horrific time she had spent in her initial captivity with him. Etienne now hoped those terrible memories would remain locked in her mind forever.

The door to the room opened and Dr. Maison came in. "What a night."

"How are the captives doing?" Etienne asked.

"Most of them were starved and dehydrated. All of

them had been beaten, but thankfully with a little tender loving care, they're all going to be okay."

"Thank God," Etienne said in relief.

"I see a makeshift bandage on your arm. What's going on?" Dr. Maison asked.

"I got shot earlier," Etienne replied.

The doctor raised an eyebrow in surprise. "Let's take a look at it." He gently unwrapped the bandage and frowned. "That's a nasty wound. You'll need to take off your shirt, so I can look at it more closely."

An hour later, Etienne walked out of the hospital, his wound cleaned out and rebandaged. He was armed with two prescriptions, one for antibiotics and one for pain. He'd fill them eventually.

He called Trey, who said that the crime scene processing was going fine and there was no reason for Etienne to return.

"We'll process your garage sometime later today, but in the meantime why don't you go home and get some rest?" Trey replied. "Seriously, Etienne, we don't need you here. Get some sleep, and I'll catch up with you later in the day."

There was one thing Etienne wanted more than sleep. He wanted answers. With this thought in mind, he headed back to the police station.

In the hallway, he bumped into Jimmy Riley, one of his officers. He told Jimmy what he wanted and then went to the interview room where Colette had spent so much time. He sank down in a chair at the head of the large table and waited.

Within minutes, Jimmy and Billy Sylvia, another one of his officers, led Brett into the room.

Brett was handcuffed, and Etienne motioned for Jimmy to take the cuffs off. The two officers then took up positions on either side of the prisoner as he sat opposite Etienne.

"The victims have all been released and are getting medical attention," Etienne said.

Brett's eyes darkened as a smirk crossed his face. "Who cares? They were nothing but swamp trash."

"Why, Brett?" Etienne leaned forward. "Help me understand why you took these people, held them and then beat and starved them."

"You'd never understand," Brett replied as a hint of anger replaced the smirk on his face.

"Try me," Etienne replied.

Brett's nostrils flared as he looked down at the table and then back up to Etienne. "This is all my father's fault. From the time I was young, he told me how wonderful the people from the swamp were. He pounded it into my head that the men and women there were stronger and smarter than I'd ever be."

Brett's anger grew. His face turned red, and his voice deepened. The words began to tumble from him furiously. "My old man loved the swamp people so much, he had an affair with a swamp whore. It destroyed my mother. Most days she didn't even get out of bed. I'd hear her crying, and I hated my father."

"I'm sorry to hear that, but what does that have to do with you taking and keeping all the victims?" Etienne asked.

"It was an experiment. I wanted to find out just how strong the swamp people really were. So I started hunting them. When I caught one, I'd drug them and take them to my basement. I beat and starved them to see how much they could take."

Brett's eyes sparked with what appeared to be pleasure. "I especially liked beating Colette. She looked so much like my father's swamp whore."

Etienne had to tamp down the rage that roared up inside him. He wanted to jump across the table and strangle the man with his bare hands for all that he had done to Colette. Instead, he rose from his chair. He had his answers, and he didn't want to look at Brett's face a minute longer.

"Cuff him and take him back to his cell," he said to the two officers.

Minutes later, Brett was gone, and suddenly sleep sounded like a good idea. Etienne had been running on empty for some time.

When he was in the emergency room, he'd asked Dr. Maison about Colette's condition. The doctor had told him she was fine. In fact, she'd already been released and had left the hospital.

Now, more than anything, Etienne wanted to go home and sleep with Colette in his arms. He wanted to hold her soft, warm body in his arms and smell the dizzying scent of her as he drifted off to sleep.

A deep relief filled him. The investigation was over, and the bad guy was finally behind bars.

Brett had been right about one thing—Etienne would

never understand his motive for what he'd done. All he knew was Brett was a deeply troubled man.

With the case solved and all the captives taken care of, Etienne just wanted Colette and dreamless sleep.

He pulled up in his driveway—but not into the garage, which was now a crime scene—and got out of the car. He walked quickly to the front door, eager to see Colette.

Unlocking the door, he went inside. "Colette?" he called out, surprised when there was no immediate reply. He went into the kitchen, but she wasn't there.

Maybe she had already gone to bed. Lord knew she'd been through plenty today. He walked down the hallway. The door to her room was open, and he peeked inside. Not only was she not there, but her bag and her clothing were gone as well.

She was really gone. Apparently, she had gone back to her shanty.

His heart dropped. She had left him without even saying goodbye. She didn't need him anymore to protect her, and her absence now spoke volumes.

The love she'd felt for him had been all about her needing him to keep her safe. Nothing more. It was what he had expected to happen, but he hadn't expected the stabbing pain in his heart.

He walked across the hallway and looked into the bathroom she had used. She'd left a small cosmetic bag behind. He'd take it to her tomorrow, and they could say their official goodbyes to each other.

His heart was heavy as he headed back to the living room. Maybe he had cared for her more than he'd wanted to admit. The house felt so empty now without her presence.

Instead of going back to his bedroom, he sank into his recliner. He had no interest in being in his bed without her there with him.

At least tomorrow he would see her once again. It would probably be the last time. That thought made his heart hurt way more than his gunshot wound.

Chapter Thirteen

Colette sat in the rocking chair in front of her shanty and watched as dawn broke overhead, painting the swamp in soft shades of gold. Morning birds began to sing from the treetops, their songs happy and bright.

However, the cheerful bird songs couldn't begin to penetrate the deep sadness that gripped Colette. She thought she'd cried all the tears she had in her, but then a new bout would overtake her, and she'd cry all over again.

She was beyond happy that the Swamp Soul Stealer had been caught. The captives had all been released and were going to be fine. But that happiness was tempered by the fact that her time with Etienne was over.

Even though she had known it was coming, despite telling herself she'd just come home and nurse her broken heart, she hadn't expected this level of heartbreak and pain.

He no longer needed her. He didn't need the memories that had flown back into her head the moment Brett had locked her in her cell once again.

She'd remembered everything then... The pain of being starved, the dizziness of dehydration, the agony of being beaten nearly every single day. It had all come rushing back to her... Everything.

However, her tears weren't because of the return of those memories. Rather, they were for the loss of Etienne. He'd been clear all along that he hadn't loved her. Oh, he'd wanted her, but he hadn't loved her.

So, just as she'd anticipated, she was home now with a broken heart.

Her love for the lawman hadn't changed. She hadn't loved him because he was protecting her. She'd fallen in love with him through their deep talks and shared laughter. She loved him for his sense of duty and his love for the town. There were a million reasons why she was in love with Etienne, but none of them mattered now.

She finally got up from the rocking chair and went through the shanty to the back deck where she started the generator.

Thank goodness, despite the late hour, Ella had been able to pick her up from Etienne's and bring her home. Colette hadn't wanted to say goodbye to Etienne. She knew she'd break down and make a complete fool of herself. It had been so much better just to leave without seeing him again.

She ate breakfast and then sat down to her computer at her desk. She wanted to lose herself in her work, so no other thoughts of Etienne would intrude into her mind.

But her mind refused to cooperate, and thoughts of the man she loved did intrude. She sat there for two hours before she gave up and turned her generator off.

By that time, it was around ten o'clock. She lay down on the sofa and closed her eyes.

She'd been so terrified when Brett grabbed her in the garage. No matter how hard she tried to get free from him, she couldn't. He hadn't run far with her before he had drugged her, and she'd fallen unconscious.

Waking up in that cell had been horrifying. It was there that her memories fully returned, slamming into her with a horrendous force. And as she had thought about suffering at the hands of Brett once again, terror had filled her.

She didn't know how long she'd been stretched out on the sofa when a knock came at the door. It was probably one of her friends. Ella had told her they were all eager to see her again.

Colette went to the door and opened it, and there he stood.

Etienne was wearing a pair of jeans and a blue polo shirt, and he looked amazingly handsome. She couldn't help the flutter of her heart at the unexpected sight of him.

"Etienne," she said.

He smiled. "Hi, Colette…do you mind if I come in for a moment?"

"Uh…okay." She stepped aside to allow him entry. She gestured him toward the sofa where they both sat.

"You forgot this last night when you packed up," he said and handed her the small cosmetic bag she'd apparently forgotten in his bathroom. So, that was why he was here. He just wanted to return her bag.

Suddenly she saw the bandage on his upper arm. "Oh, Etienne, what happened to you?"

"When we were in the garage and Brett came after you, he fired a shot and managed to hit me," he replied.

She stared at him. He'd been shot? Tears filled her eyes. He'd been shot while protecting her. Her eyes teared up, blurring her vision, and then the tears fell faster and faster down her cheeks.

"Hey, don't cry," he said. He leaned forward and wiped the tears from her cheeks. "I'm okay. The doctor even told me I was going to live," he said with a grin.

"Don't even joke about it, Etienne." She swiped at the last of her tears. "You must have been in so much pain."

He dropped his hands from her face, and his beautiful smoke gray eyes held her gaze. "Why did you leave last night?" he asked.

She leaned back from him. "I knew I was safe from the Swamp Soul Stealer... That it was over. And I knew you didn't need my memories... That you didn't need me anymore." The words came from her haltingly.

He raked a hand through his hair and released a deep sigh. His gaze was soft as it lingered on her. "I've spent all of my time with you fighting the feelings I had for you. I tried to convince myself that I didn't care about you because I was afraid once this was all over, you'd realize your feelings for me were false."

"Oh, Etienne, my feelings definitely aren't false. Don't you know? I am deeply in love with you." The words tumbled from her mouth, words she'd wanted to tell him for a long time. "I've been in love with you for some time."

"Colette, I don't need your memories, but I do need you." Oh, the gray of his eyes was so soft, so inviting. "Don't you know? I'm deeply in love with you too."

She stared at him. "For real?" she asked tremulously.

He laughed. "For real." He stood and reached for her hand, pulling her up off the sofa and into his arms. "When I got home last night and you weren't there, I was devastated. I realized then I couldn't fight my feelings for you anymore. I love you, Colette and I can't imagine my life without you in it. Thank God you're safe now. Nobody will ever hurt you again."

You're safe now. Nobody will hurt you. The soft male voice telling her she was safe and it was okay for her to open her eyes. She stared at him for a long moment as the memory suddenly leaped into her brain. The soft male voice talking to her…the soft male voice that had soothed and comforted her in the darkness.

"It was you," she whispered in stunned surprise.

He frowned. "It was me what?" he asked curiously.

"It was you who came to me in my sleep. You were there with me in the darkness of my mind."

"I sat next to you in the hospital night after night," he admitted.

She looked at him incredulously. "You talked to me. You soothed me, and I loved hearing your voice. Oh, Etienne, you were my guardian angel while I was sleeping."

He brushed his thumb gently down her cheek. "I think I fell a little bit in love with you as night after night I watched you sleep and heal. Colette, come home with me and be my wife."

Her breath caught in her throat. "I would love to be your wife, Etienne," she said as an enormous joy bloomed in her heart.

He kissed her then, a tender kiss that spoke of desire and love and a happily-ever-after with the lawman of her dreams.

Epilogue

It had been two weeks since the arrest of the Swamp Soul Stealer, and the town had breathed a deep sigh of relief. Finally, all of the vanished had left the hospital and were back where they belonged. Back with their loved ones.

Etienne sat at his desk and checked his watch. It was almost five o'clock, almost time for him to leave and head home. Home. The house had never felt so warm, so embracing as it did now with Colette in it.

Thank goodness the crime in Crystal Cove had returned to such things as speeding and shoplifting. Nothing serious had come across his desk, and he hoped it stayed that way forever.

Without the Swamp Soul Stealer taking up all the hours of the day, Etienne now had the time to walk the streets and speak with people.

Apparently, the recall efforts had died with Brett's incarceration. Etienne knew the people in Crystal Cove were behind him and supporting him and that made him want to work harder than ever for them.

A knock fell on his door. "Come in," he called out.

Trey came in and sat in the chair across from Etienne's desk. "I figured I'd catch up with you before you headed home."

"Is there something going on that needs my attention?" Etienne asked with dread.

"Absolutely nothing," Trey replied with a grin.

"Damn, you had me worried there for a minute," Etienne replied.

"Isn't it nice that things have been so quiet lately?" Trey said.

"Yeah, it's nice, and let's hope things stay quiet," Etienne replied. "I'm getting ready to leave and go home."

"You know, I've never seen you as happy as you've been since you have Colette in your life."

"I've never been as happy as I am now," Etienne admitted. "She has brought me such happiness, and I can't wait to marry her."

"Are you two making wedding plans?" Trey asked curiously.

"Absolutely. We just want a simple ceremony in front of a judge. She's asked Ella Gaines to be her maid of honor, and I would like it if you would be my best man."

"Oh, wow. I'd be honored," Trey said with a surprised smile.

"Great. I'll let you know the date when we've decided on one. Trust me, it's going to be very soon, and on that note, it's time for me to go home to my bride-to-be." Etienne got up from his desk, and Trey stood as well.

"Then I'll just see you in the morning," Trey said as the two men stepped out into the hallway.

"See you then," Etienne replied.

Minutes later, Etienne was in his car and headed

home. A sweet anticipation filled him as he thought of the woman waiting for him there.

Some people might say they were in the honeymoon of their relationship, but that wasn't true. Etienne's love for her was deep and abiding. He recognized now that he had loved her for a long time. Fear had kept him from seeing his love for her. He'd been afraid to embrace that love, afraid that she would realize she wasn't in love with him.

He wasn't afraid anymore, and he'd never been so happy. He pulled into the driveway and opened the garage, which had finally been cleared for Etienne to use once again. He parked inside and stepped from the garage into the kitchen.

Colette turned from the stove and smiled. "Hi, Chief Savoie."

As always, she looked pretty in a pair of jeans and a brown blouse that perfectly matched her chocolate-colored eyes. Her luxurious hair was loose down her back.

"Hello, Ms. Broussard. Something smells delicious in here," he said and took her in his arms.

She smiled up at him. "That would be chicken cacciatore. How was your day?"

"Fairly boring."

"And that's the way we like them, right?" she said, her eyes sparkling brightly.

"How was your day?" he asked.

"I sold an article."

"Colette, that's great," he exclaimed, knowing how much it meant to her.

"You know what's really great? Sharing my news with the man I love. And I do love you, Etienne."

His heart warmed at her words...words he would never tire of hearing from her. First, she'd been a sleeping beauty he wanted to awaken. Then she'd been a woman who needed his protection. Now she was the woman he loved more than anything or anyone in the world.

"I love you too," he replied and then took her lips with his in a kiss that held all the love, all the desire he felt for her. He knew they shared a love that would see them through life for many years to come.

* * * * *

Look for more swamp stories from
New York Times *bestselling author Carla Cassidy*
coming soon!